Family Romance

visuals by Nick Patterson

verbals by Tom Bradley

baubobooks.org

baubobooks.org

*Now go and smite the Amalekites,
and utterly destroy all that they have,
and spare them not; but slay both
man and woman, infant and suckling,
ox and sheep, camel and ass.*

—I Samuel 15:3

i.

"Cover your face with both hands when you sneeze. You never know when a pathogen has fastened on your head."

That's Mom talking. As usual she's forcing herself on us and in us. She must control our reflex motions. Mom must micro-manage the gases and moisture that exit our faces. She gets fidgety and unfulfilled unless occupying others' sinuses and limbs, the gluttoness.

I object to being materfamiliassed by a creature so ravenous (if intermittently shapely). And I'm sure my dear siblette would agree, if the sad child were still able to mull more than a semi-no-tion inside what remains of her mind.

As for the more explicitly testicular of our par-ents—who knows where absent Dad would come down on this issue? Mom and pathogens are the sole topics he's reluctant to discuss in secret letters from across the Judeuphrates, where has defected to please himself behaving like a traitor/apostate among the Relict Amalekites.

In Dad's absence, Mom's favorite way to rape us of self-possession is immune system anx-iety. She has taken the germ theory and twisted it into pre-moistened masochist porn. Her term for any well-being threat is "pathogen."

Not just bacteria and viruses, not merely lice and tapeworms, but—

psychosomatosis,
connective tissue sprain,
clinical depression,
poor social connectivity,

sulphurous flatulence,
scrotal and/or labial fatigue from excessive
"maestrobation"
(as she taught us to mispronounce it)—

—all of these are brought on by pathogens. This is according to the fascist conjuress whom we are expected to call, for lack of a less inappropriate moniker, *Mom.*

And yet, in spite of the pan-systemic pathogens that lurk everywhere, she was somehow persuaded (presumably by her opposite number) to grunt me out into this world, and to perform the same disservice for my emotionally vegetative little sissy. One after the other, Mom extruded the pair of us. She dragged our naked spirits down from the gritty smogma overhead and enfleshed us, emboned us, left us to languish dadlessly on the planetary crust, bug-vulnerable and liable at any moment to succumb to—

the Sneeze Catastrophic.

The nurturing instinct in our remaining parent is not so much hypertrophied as sarcastic. Even in this epoch of worldly war and widespread privation, she prettifies us. She somehow scrounges the means to bring about lovely coiffures high upon our occupied heads, all the better for her unwellness vectors to perch and nest. She gussies us up in off-the-shoulder love-sarongs, thick in fiber, subtropical in batik.

(I don't know about my sweet little siblette's, but it seems likely the weft of my particular garment has an ulterior warp.)

You won't be surprised to hear that Mom prettifies her pet sick-makers, too, before siccing them on us. Such organisms are too precious to flit around in plain brown wraps. A typical Mom-bug will boast not only feathery antennae, but glamorous pseudo-eyes on its wings.

Mom dresses us in off-the-shoulder love-sarongs

In much the same way, Doers of the Churchy-Stately Behaviors will tart themselves up in the whole-body spandex chasuble before yanking felonious blasphemers' armpits inside-out. Little Sister once fell afoul of the Municipal Priestcrafters, and if she could mouth more than a half-dozen toddler locutions these days, she'd tell you all about—

the dread civil/sacral strappado.

All mothers want their non-girlish whelps to cling like an acetate nightie to sex-wet thighs. And, if you are a canny expunger of incipient virility, you know the best way to promote clinginess is to live in a neighborhood where something offputting happens every time your un-daughter slips out to perform the backyard chores.

clergy-brutes fixing to give my sister a seeing-to

ii.

I am expected each dawn, noon and dusk to go out and collect calories. This is an atavism from our former status as an—

Amniobaptismo-Certified Regimental Ménage of the Endogamous Bellicose Caste, Cavalrous Subdivision.

The eldest spawn of a Cavalryman is the designated forager, according to martial/canonical law as divinely revealed in those glorious days before whatever took place a long time ago was supposedly going on.

When I say we are—rather, before the paternal abandonment, *were*—an amniobaptismically certified ménage of the regimental category, I wonder if it's possible to emphasize strongly enough the extent and depth to which the quartet of us once fit into that relatively lofty socio-nook.

I suppose the starting question should be how we became a family, with a lower-case *eff*, in the first place. How in the name of our Exclusive National/Racial Redeemer-God—

the divine Krystelle Rex

—did someone so reputedly unsickish as Dad ever get infected by a syndrome of such virulent pathogens as have been wadded together and mis-nomered "Mom"?

I'm told the pair met, time gone by, at—where else?—a gala defense industry expo. The venue of their first love-sighting was a vast convention center in the Riparian Megalopolis, within shooting distance of what was to become our dining room.

within shooting distance

Soon-to-be-Dad, still young and green in judgment, was a hereditary recruit in the ceremonial Mounted Corps. He seems to have been born with a Cavalryman's plasma osmosing through his various connective tissues, which is convenient, because enrollment in that august body happens to be his inborn lot in civic life. (Mine, too, pointlessly enough.)

But violence zaps through his muscles as well. This renders him unsuited for the decorative function to which the saddle-straddling soldiery have degenerated over the millennia. Dad requested leave from his platoon to engage in warcraft—or at least vicariously to experience state-sanctioned genocide via the magic of stagecraft.

So he landed a gig as a corporate mascot at the expo. In full entomo-mechano drag, on cue, he was paid to come looming and shrieking from a backlit phosphorus explosion. He promised satisfactory levels of pugnacity to bulk purchasers of a powerful biocidal agent marketed under a now-famous brand name. Here's the pitch he recited while trundling around the dais, trying to look lethal:

Our product is being applied to great effect in the Middling Orient. It's specially formulated to liquefy the strange yet probably sentient rind of the Relict Amalekites, who were supposed to have been genocided like a freckle off the flaking face of the planet way back in scato-scriptural times.

Dad landed a gig as corporate mascot.

Their tenaciousness is only surpassed by their furtiveness, as they make like bandy-legged Bedou among the grit dunes on the perpetually disputed far bank of the Judeuphrates. Your vaunted "Sovereign Ecclesiarchy," under the sway of the Grand Religiopath, intends to complete the grim chore this time around, and to smite these vermin once and for all, with the help of—

(electronic rhythm-box roll...)

Flamma-Manna

It just occurred to me that you might get the wrong idea about Dad from the above. Shall I provide you, now, with an utterance on the same subject from this individual in his maturity?

Here's something direct and recent from his pen, as opposed to a script he memorized as a youth for a pittance. For further geopolitical background, I refer you to this secret letter which a wiser Dad dispatched from an encampment dug into the "grit dunes," camouflaged under the poisoned and smoldering fronds of a stunted, isolated date palm. (Incidentally, I am not prepared at this point to reveal how this lethal correspondence comes before my eyes; you're free to suspect a foolhardy, suicidal and/or bribed postman.)

Your Sovereign Ecclesiarchy's stillborn conscience, in the person of the Grand Religiopath, saw fit to unleash agony and melting death upon the Relict Amalekites' first line of defense—namely, their epidermis. Hence illiberal applications of Flamma-Manna were decreed, toward the promotional marketing of which, it mortifies me to admit, I once stumbled around in a clown suit. I am trying to make amends today, with saddle sores and bubbling skin on the more exposed parts of me.

It floats whitely down from the sky to no pleasant effect, this Flamma-Manna, causing civilians to scurry thitherward in their fuddled masses.

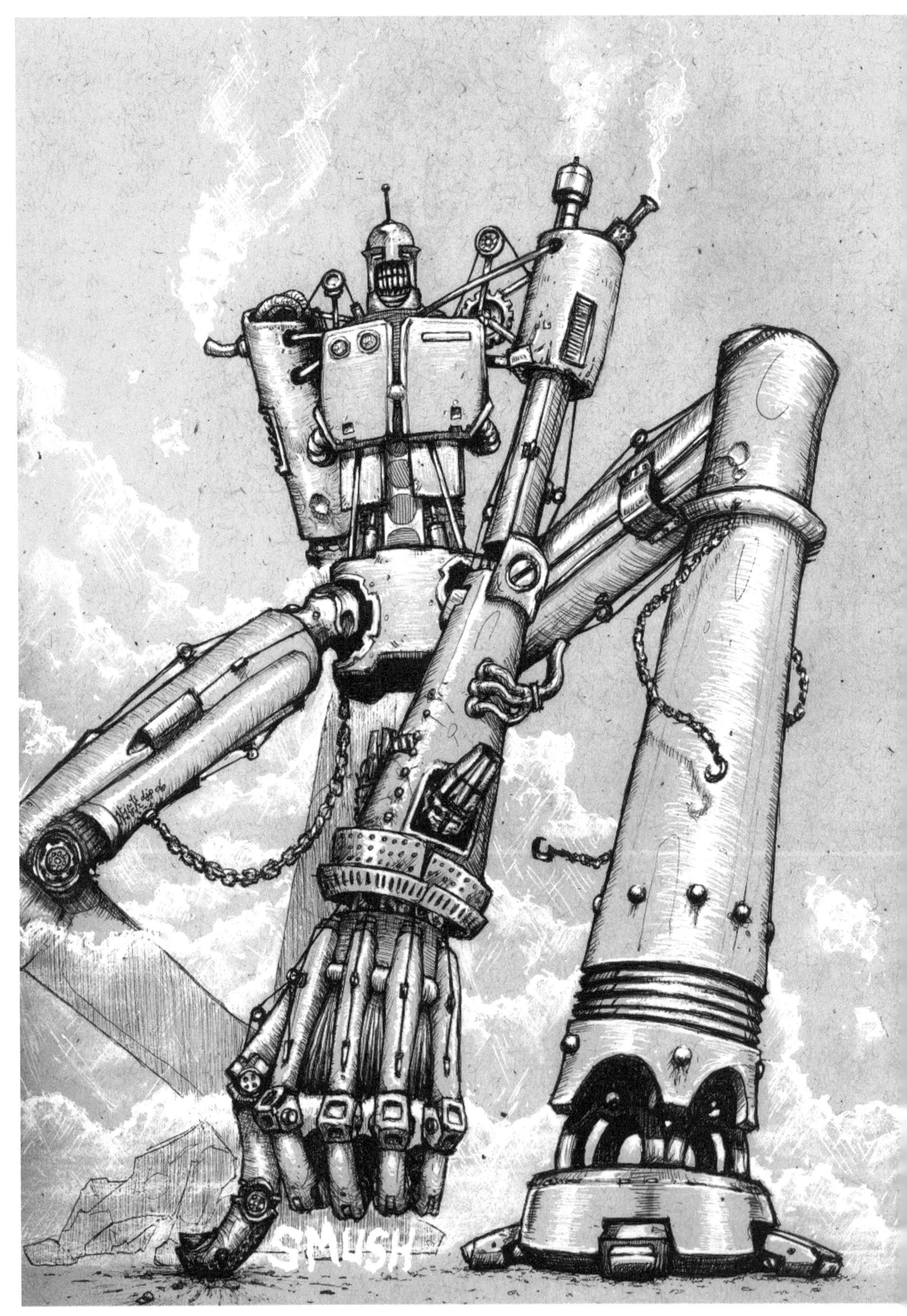

Weapon of Sparse Destruction

But I, even though dismissed by your neighbors as a mere "skeddadling bolter," am by nature obdurate enough to stick it out. I've come to enjoy the bracing sting, like a slap on the face with chilled astringent of a suburban morning.

The Grand Religiopath's justification for this biocide is that "vegetative cover needs to be removed" (it's the most barren sediment in the world) to aid his search for the notorious Weapon of Sparse Destruction. This ostensible techno-abomination is believed to be capable of long-range surgical strikes. Precision comes with the package precisely because the destruction is so sparse.

If it existed, the contrivance would be the very definition of inefficiency. Still, that design defect would add zero plausibility to the ludicrous claim that it could, in a thousand years, have been developed by an ethno-species which is barely lingual, much less technological.

Might it be too cynical to suspect that the whole murderous enterprise is being dumped on my head as a marketing ploy, a promo campaign for a certain redundant defoliant?

* * * *

Meanwhile, backwards in what is sometimes called *spacio-temporality*, pre-Mom (whose attitudes toward foreigners of any stripe never mellowed with maturity) was working the punters at the gala defense industry expo as a double-threat taxi dancer/vintage weapons demonstratrix. In the latter role, her stage designation was—

Equestrienne Princess of the Month

Of course, only a lass of her Endogamous Bellicose Caste background could qualify for such an honorific. And it seems to have suited her at the time, for she was still relatively fresh and naked in her maidenly incarnation (such as it was).

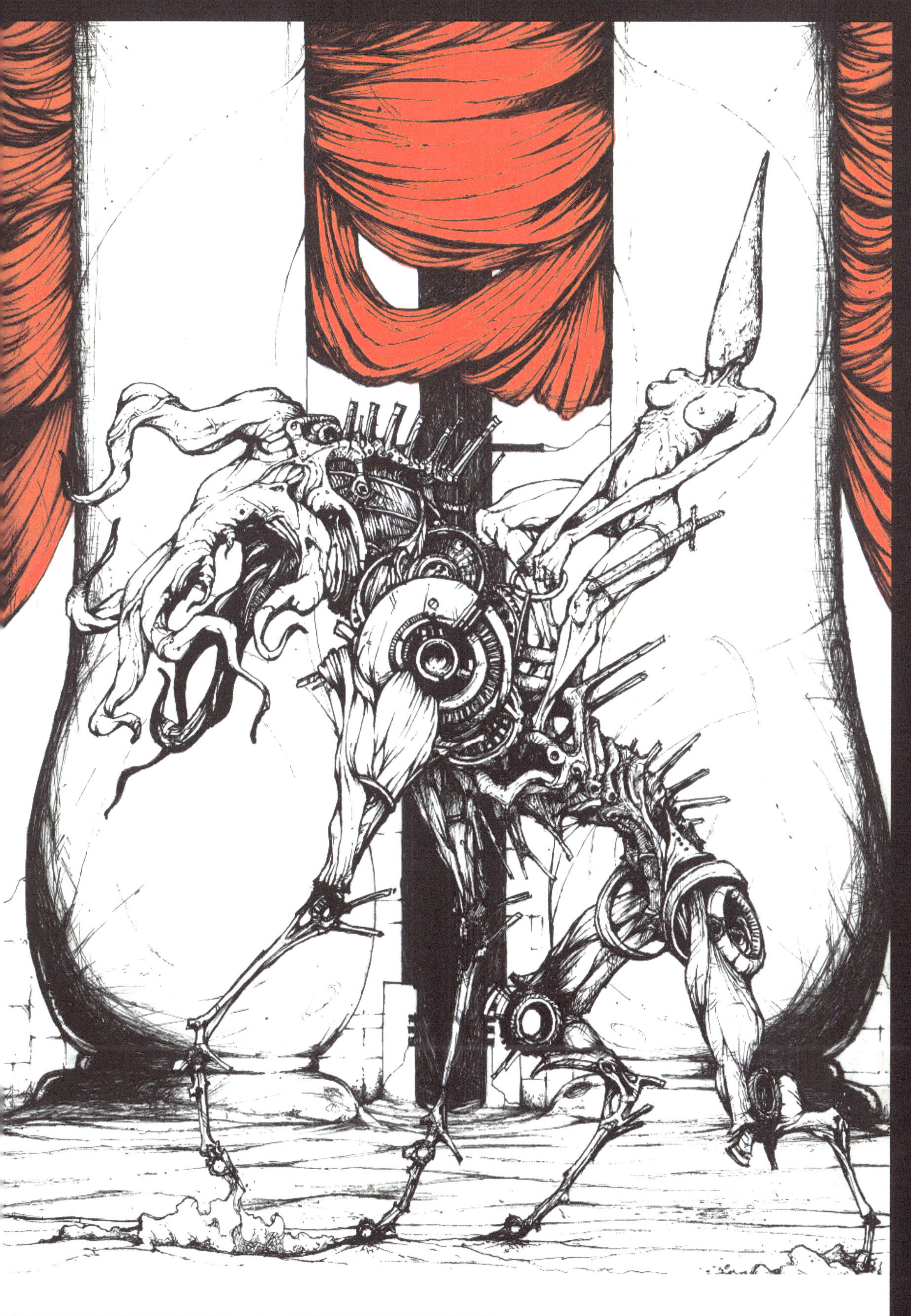

*Mom's formidable vagina points out
the excellence of her urban assault vehicle.*

As Dad lumbered about in his mascot costume, he kept one eye on this royalty, and was wowed by her performance. Particularly beguiling was the manner in which she employed her formidable vagina as a pointing device to indicate her ride's excellent vertebral development.

It was one of those quaintly dated odd-toed ungulates which were brought so stylishly into existence during the bygone era, with such simple pugnacity as to appeal to the sentimental hearts of all war-makers, mounted or un-. It pranced double time, with the precision of a Lipizzaner and the footedness of a Clydesdale. Dad marveled as Mom clanked and cantered her galvanized gelding among the patrio-pious bunting, a bayonet phallused to her flexi-femur, a symbolically penisoid dunce cap erected on her pate, shaven for the occasion.

Their shifts over, both pretty youngsters having ducked behind the blood-red satin billows, one of my prospective parents made haste to un-thigh the other from the trotter. In the process he is assumed to have blastulated the scion who, in the future, *this* future, would birth the illuminated romance which you presently hold in your hands, instead of keeping those extremities freed up, at the ready, fingers extended, should an unwellness vector flutter off these bled pages and insinuate a Sneeze Catastrophic upon the frontal portion of your head.

I say Dad is *assumed* to have blastulated me behind the bunting. This is not my, but rather society's default assumption, Mom being my "mom" and all. I suspect virgin birth—if that's not too presumptuous. If his breath were bearable, it might be useful to consult my father's grandly religiopathological nemesis on the matter.

* * * *

And when, of course, in the blink of an eye, the time came for marital warfare to be waged, so inevitable in these times of regimental rot and declining troop morale, Dad not only forsook his brand-new, freely chosen wife, but he went AWOL from his immemorially and genetically predetermined branch of the armed services. He abandoned the household which he'd been simultaneously born and conscripted to defend, and he turned his muscly back on our Inseparable Church-State as well, along with its synonymous race and coextensive land mass. I believe this is called—

"quite a step in one's personal development."

It was the sheer excellence of Mom's demonstration that led to the loss of the very hubby she gained by it. To her chagrin, it turned out not to be herself but her ride that he hankered to centaurize onto. Some hubbies are driven away by their wifeys; our paterfamilias was ridden off by himself. He *became one*, as they say, with the very odd-toed ungulate which the Equestrienne Princess of the Month had vaginated so ably at the expo. (Shall we say he requisitioned it for an unspecified period of time?)

Dad became one with the odd-toed ungulate.

Some grooms ride their brides. Dad groomed his ride. The two of them, like a disembodied spirit and its energumen, rode to the banks of the Judeuphrates and waded across, straight into the peculiarly shaped arms whose flesh he'd helped to dissolve with his sales pitch.

* * * *

The Relict Amalekites are among the planet's few political entities quaint enough to maintain a mounted force in anything more than a decorative capacity. Seeing as how their average crotch is better adapted for squatting and shitting on the ground than hemorrhoiding on a government-issue saddle, this quaintness could be interpreted as a fine example of idiotic backwardness. It might even have something to do with how easeful our Inseparable Church-State is finding their extermination—rather, "smiting" is the term which the Grand Religiopath says we should prefer. It sounds more authoritative, I suppose, coming from received scato-scripture.

Regarding the absent entity once hailed in our dining room with the three-letter capital-D word, a cynical supposition has been hissing through the

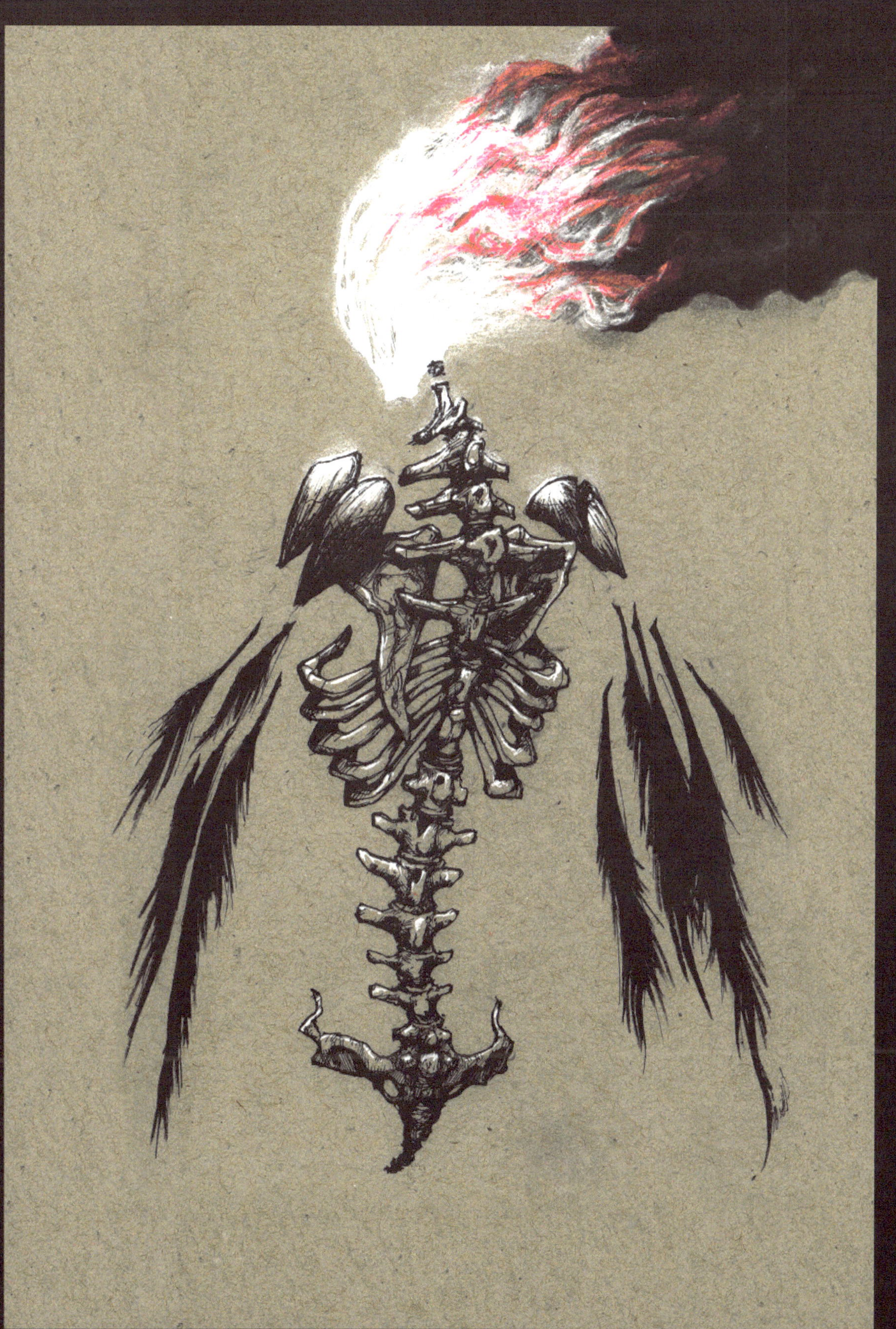

Flamma Manna floats whitely down
from the sky, to no pleasant effect.

Riparian Megalopolis. It is said that neither politics nor pity, but merely love of galloping, cantering and trotting caused Dad to vanish with spurs and bridle.

For whatever reason, Dad has exiled himself in the un-Krystelle Rexed, hence damned quadrant of our planet, where no grass sprouts underfoot, just drifts of hoof-eroding minerals and jags of crystal shards, where no branchy things spring up, because, three paces beyond the not infrequently dry riverbed, there's never ambient fluid enough to engender the sort of fecundity that flops, green and fungal, from Nature's pudenda.

The Relict Amalekites' Middlingly Oriental homeland is the sort of grim purgatory where, if non-girlish offspring were sent out each dawn, noon and dusk to gather calories, they would return with nothing to eat but glops of their own fingertips, melted to red biocided mush.

And if I, seed of a "skittering tergiversator" and "blabbermouth sharer of pugnacio-tech," still forage prior to every meal, it's for a platoon whose lieutenant fragged off long ago.

iii.

Besides scrounging for nutriment, I engage in another atavistic behavior thrice daily. With the mindless regularity of an autonomic nervous tic, I join my pater-challenged family in pre-meal devotional grovels to our Exclusive National/Racial Redeemer-God—

the Divine Krystelle Rex

The exposure of Our Savior's pathogen-ridden condition appeals to Mom's prayerful sensibility. It's a gesture of piety on her part to dress us like him. Mom learned about the love-sarong, thick in fiber, from the Divine Krystelle Rex, for he, too, was once swaddled by his own problematically parthenogenic Madonna, and given a hermaphroditic name to go with the look.

"But," Mom recites by rote from Holy Porno-Writ before we dip sporks in bowls, "when the time for immolation came, our Vicarious Atoner was compelled, in the name of humiliation, to roll down his immaculate love-sarong. He furled it from off-the-shoulder to just-above-pubis. The exposure mortified our Redeemer more than the elbow-chains and worms pained him. This we can tell from soberly pondering the Divine Krystelle Rex's facial expression in our battalion-issue representationalistic splatter-icon—"

She holds up the graphic in question. We pause, sporks poised, soberly to meditate upon the mortified Physiognumen. He did have a bit of a tummy on him.

How will he cover his face with both hands?

Back in my little sister's long-gone lingual days, before she fell prey to this deity's bureau of clergy-brutes, she would interrupt the pre-meal devotional with panicky sounds that should have forewarned us of brain disasters in the offing. In my recurring nightmare-memories of mealtimes, Sissy always shudders these words:

"Sad God looks like he's just about to make the Sneeze Catastrophic! See how he sucks in! But how will he be able to cover his face with both—"

Unable to finish her question, my beloved siblette begins to bray like an underbred odd-toed ungulate.

Mom ignores her younger issue's ominous sounds and directs us to consider the Divine Krystelle Rex's worms, his elbow chains. We avert our eyes from his shamefully down-rolled love-sarong, all the while trying to ignore, too, the unoccupiedness of Dad's stool at the head of the food table.

Even if the latter wasn't across the river these days, he would be pointedly absent from this devotional. If I might not exactly share it, at least I can relay his contempt for this so-called "Vicarious Atoner" of ours. In one of his letters secretly dispatched from the trans-Judeuphrates, where he rides in the cavalry of a rival deity, Dad has discharged his spiritual arsenal thus:

Kryssie-poo was up to either elbow in junior adjutants, which doesn't say a whole lot. Do you think they chainifixed and wormolated him/her on no charge whatever? His/her mitts were cauterized

at the wrist-knobs for mutual maestrobation with a minor mammaloid.

Sure, it was a time of social chaos. But guess who behaved worse than anybody. Why do you think li'l Kryssie got a spanking almost as exquisite as the one I'm in for if I ever cross over again?

If the Grand Religiopath ever re-corkscrewed his venomous tongue into me, it would make the passion of your godlet look like a junior princess-style birthday party. (Tell your tiny fellow inmate I can't make it this year, either.)

Please do "soberly ponder" the asinine "facial expression" in that "battalion-issue representationalistic splatter-icon" your mother flaps in your face before letting you continue your slow death by malnutrition. Look at that lusty mouth on him/her. You can tell Miss Divine Kryssie-pooters repented at the last minute, because he/she was ashamed of finding his/her martyrdom so toothsome. That's no Disastrous Achoo on that mug. It's a sploogi-simper.

If they really wanted to punish this exhibi-tionistic masochist, they'd chainifix and wormolate him/her in a dark room rather than a major Ripar-ian Megalopolitan street corner. Or they'd at least pull that love-sarong up to modest off-the-shoulder level.

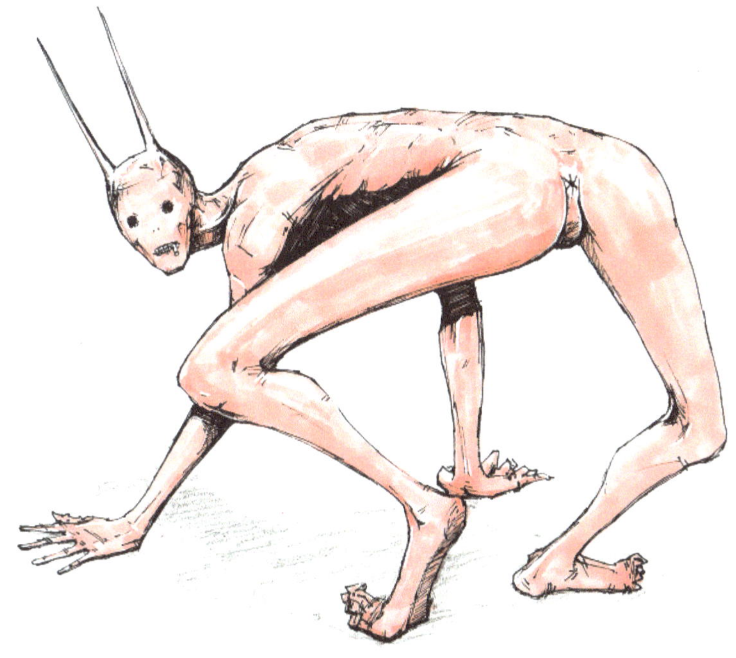

unsheathed in the sacred chasuble

When I say, "they," of course, I mean practi-tioners of Priestcraft, who are the same in all times

39

and places, and under all banners, regardless of the alias, fake nose and rhinestone bathrobe that gets provisionally slapped onto the Single Universal Bloated Emanation they all serve. Had the planet been cursed with his presence in those days, The Grand Religio-fucking-path would have been among the first to drill a worm into your Redeemer's deflated love handles.

Are you aware of how much less imposing that Highest of High Physio-Functionaries looks when he's not sheathed in the sacred chasuble? There's a lot more to that vestment than spandex. Enough underwires to secure a concentration camp.

That's why I like it here: no theocrats, no clerical apparatchiks of any kind, and never have been since scato-scriptural times. Just a direct line to their particular dada in the sky, who seems less meddlesome than most, having written everything out beforehand and taken an especially long nap, or something. I'm not paying a whole lot of attention to that, and nobody expects me to.

Merely to harbor a phrase or two of this content on the premises would earn for our entire household the same horrendous punitive sentence that Dad faces if he comes home for a birthday, or for any other reason.

And, of course, as I'm sure you know already (if only on the molecular level), the horrendous punitivity of that sentence is what, eventually, ensures—

my begetter's inevitable comeback.

* * * *

Habit's a strong force. Here's what I hymn when pondering the Passion of the Rex. As I go outside to exploit our single culinary resource, I sing, in the dead-ish liturgical lingo of our deoxyribo-politico-nucleic faith—

Pluck forth thy coiffure's pathogens,

pluck forth thy locks entwined within,

pluck forth from radiant brows the flesh

which pads the seams where headbones mesh.

Pry back thy scalp like fecund sod,

expose thy rank mind's fungal pods,

chip free thy skull, let marrow drain

till one grey tegument remains.

And when thy brain is amply shown,

and naught is left of skin and bone,

*then serve thyself to **KRYSTELLE REX**,*

or suffer our collective hex.

Three Horsemen of the Trial Separation

I've heard it's not unusual for estranged parents to recruit their progeny as both weapons and battleground. In our case the militarism is naturally exaggerated, by virtue of the endogamous caste under which we are subsumed. Dad being exiled from, and we abiding in our Inseparable Church-State, the Family Romance becomes nothing less than micro-geopolitical. And, in a Sovereign Ecclesiarchy such as the one we abide in, spousal strife takes on an automatic religiosity: distaff piety caught in a strategic struggle with agnate blasphemy.

My little sister and I will either snap in this tug-o'-war, or the contestants will mutually self-destroy. Our generation will be the only bits remaining on the battlefield, a doubly frayed bit of rope, looking like a two-headed serpent coiled, or maybe just tangled, on the dining room rug.

iv.

So, a trio of times daily, under the invisible super-vision of our chainifixed and wormolated Savior, I mash down my coiffure so as not to look ridic-ulous, doff my love-sarong for the same reason, don some dungarees, and perform the immemorial chore of a Cavalryman's eldest offspring. It's sim-plified because, like those of so many single par-ents, our Mom's menu is encompassed by a unitary dish. Bowl, rather.

At the foot of our food table each morning, noon and night she stands, having laid aside the battalion-issue splatter pic. Before we are permitted to lower sporks into our contra-nutritious meal of one ingredient, Mom must proclaim words to this effect:

"All upper-mammaloids capable of choice should choose but a single substance to subsist upon and ask for no more, in order to avoid differential pathogens. And, my youngsters, what is the second of the three reasons we maintain obsessional monophagy?"

the Designated Forager

Mom pauses for us to supply the response, which I never do, for my own civil-sacral safety. Sometimes Sissy, whose head is no longer capable of harboring the self-preservation instinct, manages, via some neural-phonetic memory/reflex, to splutter out the ten required syllables:

"To postpone planetary depletion."

Any member of the baptizenry would be forgiven for flattening him/her/itself on the rug at the sound of that phrase. Juxtaposing the words "planetary" and "depletion" is canonically prosecutable within the borders of a religio-political entity whose sole contribution to world culture is the most powerful biocide ever brewed.

Fearless Mom continues her utterance in an even more perilous vein: "Yes, and just as importantly, we subsist monosubstantially to express dietary solidarity with our tragic victims on the trans-Judeuphrates bank."

Such dangerous talk would come as a surprise from any baptizen. But it's particularly unexpected

the expected civil servant

from someone who was ditched in those tragic victims' favor, whose estranged hubby happens to be galloping along parched wadis, at the head of an unsuitably crotched cavalry, under the banner of their debunked rival deity. (I balk from introducing that bugaboo's blasted name to your ear.) Has she forgotten that she is known as the ex-fellow-bedder of a nullifidian runagate, condemned in absentia to slow strangulation by means of his own intestines if he should ever set foot again in his homeland? (No wonder Dad misses all our birthdays.)

When she talks dirty like this, venting blasphemo-treason at the top of her shapely lungs, Mom makes sure the dining room window sash is flung wide to whoever or whatever might be eavesdropping and voyeuring. It seems as though this naked, self-destructive being hankers for a house call from the ever-expected civil servant who will put an end to our already twenty-five percent fragmented Family Romance once and for all.

What about the rind being bubbled
off their dear siblettes?

She has caused it to be murmured around the Riparian Megalopolis that our household has adopted monophagia because she hears a "planetary cry of agony" every time a new batch of Flamma-Manna is urged upon our enemies.

"Each time we dump all over the Middling Orient," she rants and shrieks as the three of us huddle around the four-seater food table, "another quasi-comestible is rendered extinct within the envirulence of the long-suffering Relict Amalekites, and hence an ala carte item is erased from their ever dwindling menu. Is this just? Is this wholesome?"

"Menu curtailment, what an injustice!" I scoff, even though sarcasm works as well on her as sulphuric acid on glass. "What about the rind being bubbled off their dear siblettes?"

Little Sissy writhes with empathy. She vocalizes and strains against her food chair straps. I hate to exacerbate the miserable tenor of my co-generationalist's existence, but I must emphasize my point, meanwhile looking at and listening to her with care.

"We smite them and our poison settles down on the gummy sand to irritate their sweet little sissies' nasal passages and make them do the Sneeze Catastrophic. Just imagine that."

"Should we, then," continues Mom, ignoring my interruption and her younger issue's tongue-swallowing ictus, "luxuriate in a multifarious diet replete with sauces and fructo-sorbets between courses? Monophagia can be the only fit expression of our politico-ethno-churchificial chagrin."

She fills our bowls with bits of a particular non-sentient entity which has, not uncoincidentally, begun to flourish in our backyard with unprecedented rankness since the commencement of hostilities.

V.

The debiologification is happening so far away that you will be excused for not believing Mom's story about hearing agony-cries from such a distance—especially since she's lying.

Her nutritional *idée fixe* is indeed a response to hearing the plops of something being dropped on the "planetary epidermis." But it's an altogether different substance, and it's flopping down much closer to home.

Not unlike Flamma-Manna, this stuff's deposition is a direct result of the current state of worldly war. But it smells even worse than a military-industrial poison, and, in fact, promotes the lushest vomiting forth of useful vegetation.

It's not being shat from machinery, but is rather extruded from the problematical recta of creatures who have colonized our backyard. You could say the percussions of warfare have jostled them to flock to the rear of our house, where they molt and roost. Or maybe I should say they shed and squat, for these ornitho-plantigrade viviparoids (roughly speaking) are performing the second verb in more than one way. More squatters than roosters, in fact.

And, incidentally, they have, indeed, been hanging around the flung-wide sash of our dining room window, eavesdropping and voyeuring, at least to the extent their bestial levels of consciousness permit such sophisticated behaviors.

Meanwhile, they generate an exploitable resource right under the pertinent windowsill. Thus is promoted the monoculture of breakfast, lunch and supper (eucharist, too), to be conveniently and cost-effectively gatherable by the non-girl of the

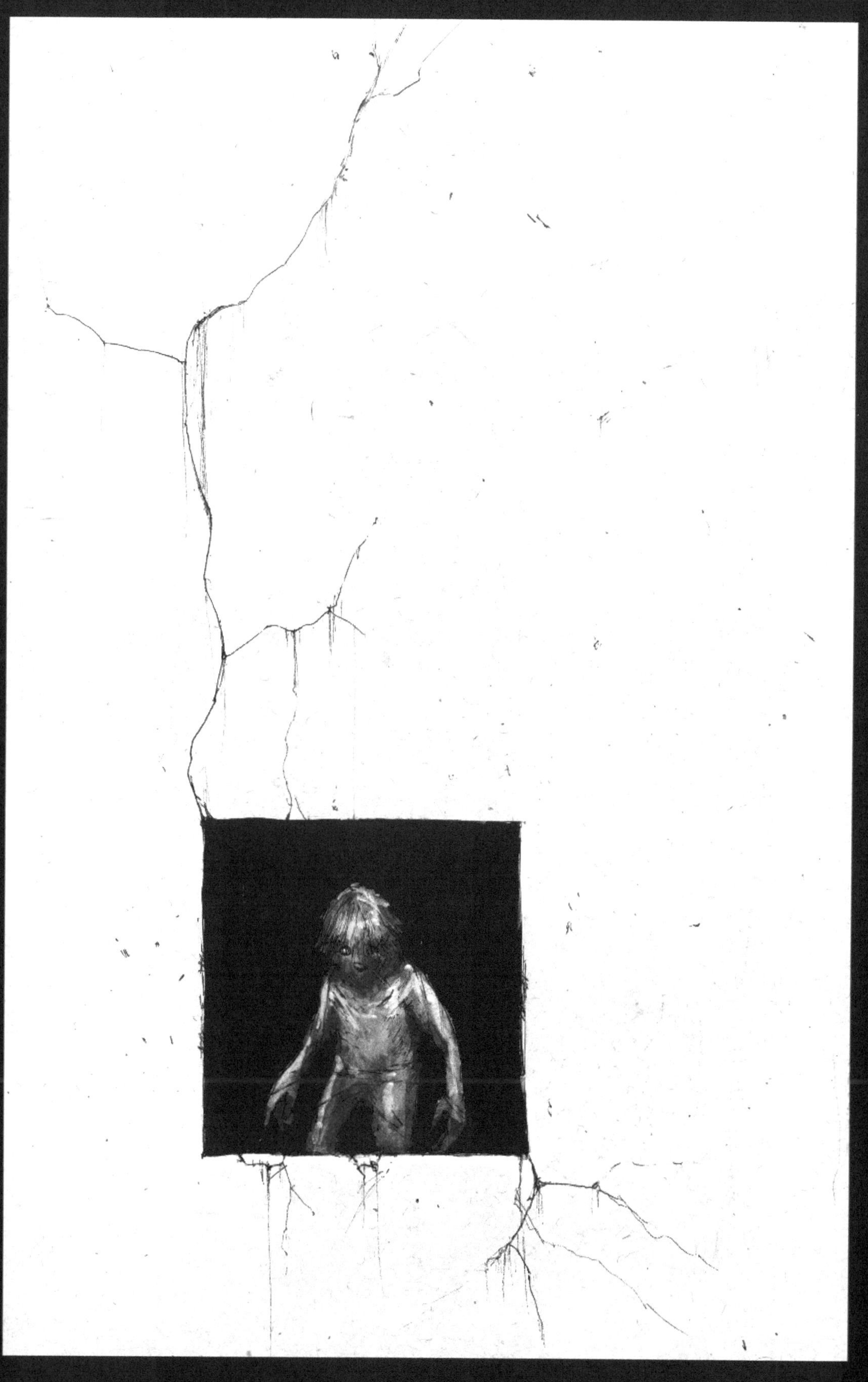

*My sister hasn't the temerity to
peek out behind the house.*

house, the foraging Cavalryman's eldest spawn, the narrator of this Family Romance.

* * * *

Sissy harbors certain elaborate and unshakeable delusions with regard to the physical appearance of the infesters and beshitters of the place where she used to gambol before losing her *rationis capax*. She believes she can sense them peeking, listening to Mom's blasphemo-treasonable shrieks, and jotting copious Palmer-Methodical notes (absurdest implausibility of all, as you'll soon see), to be folded four ways and postal-delivered into the claws of the same Grand Religiopath who long ago licked away her hymen as well as her capacity for sequential thought.

Sissy claims the ability to see, or at any rate to mentate these uninvited guests through the wallpaper, sheetrock and stucco. No doubt she's suppressing and projecting differentially configured

where she used to gambol

certain inaccurate notions about our squatters.

demons, who represent something unrelated, if no less horrible, and who autonomously haunt the labyrinthine convolutions of her decentralized nervous endings.

She has never had the temerity actually to look out and try to catch a glimpse, and she can't have actually seen their big plumage, bigger hands and arguable crotches. But however her mind's warped cornea interprets their imaginary aspect, I don't doubt my sister apprehends our unhappy campers' moral and spiritual reality with absolute clarity, like rat corpses phosphorescing among splintery joists.

I do realize and regret that my brief thrice-daily sallies among these wretches constitute desertion of our tiny lunatic, when, for no better reason than to stave off family starvation, I must leave my sicklier counterpart at the mercy of unwellness vectors and other elaborate motherly whims.

But Sissy would die of a brain spasm if she were even to consider following me out of Mom's eclipse and into the crawling, clamoring company of her outdoor terrors.

outdoor terrors

vi.

It's only through reluctant effort that I recall a time when, like the earlier version of Dad, I too was up to my pube-line in warmish fluid. It's with placentimentality that I try to reestablish in my mind the mood of the moment when I was too young to be punished for ipsism-qua-bedwetting in a pungent yet mollifying semen-urine blend, and could luxuriate awash in something resembling the Judeuphrates' exfoliatory saline solution.

I am speaking, of course, of having adherence to the ancestral sect imposed on me via the extraordinary expedient of intrauterine lavage, i.e.,

amniobaptism

amniobaptism. This is how the deterministic life-death sentence of the Endogamous Bellicose Caste gets foisted.

Given the creepily implied Mom-proximity, it is with agonized reluctance and edge-ground teeth that I entertain such a dim memory of my ur-self, and assume this element to have been the cloying syrup in which the prenatal trauma must be relived.

It's as though my angle of vision is furnished through the meatus of one of those viddy-cams poised in the glans of an endo-stalk, whose tubularity gets screwed into the (as it were) *landlady's* umbilicus, in order to spelunk the ribbed mater-vault.

Karma, they say, is the mere handmaiden of heredity. I seem to have forded this figurative Judeuphrates before Dad blinked off the glint in his eye that blastulated me, before he absconded with the odd-toed ungulate to be a contractor or whatever among our deoxyribo-politico-nucleic enemies.

And in my deja vulva I am fetal in some half-hatched manner, so inexperienced as to smile at someone out of the frame who hasn't yet violated that smile, as all eventually must. The river and sky are emblematic of a maniacal mater's innards, and there is neither backyard nor spying squatters to meconiumize it.

shock-vergers

Most survivors recollect as peaceful and comfy their spell awash in the endometriotic retch-sauce. You won't be surprised to hear that you-know-who spoiled that for me, in the name of pathogen-siccing. Already she was on the job, even before her poison broke.

She inserted a pessary, and thereby dispatched an aborto-virus to swim after me, like one of our Inseparable Church-State's conscripted shock-vergers chasing my Dad, trying to put an end to him before he can muck all the way across to the far bank and baste under the ostensible beneficence of the Middlingly Oriental Competitor Creator.

This pessary was infested with the kind of aborto-virus that turns the peritoneal waterway bile-yellow with its approach, and was prescribed in a lubricated bolus by, of course, our Diocesan-Trained Familopath and comic relief—

Crusty ol' Doc Clyster.

But Mom only dispatched a semi-competent one. She did not want to procure good and proper miscarriage, just a half-incapacitated pup, like

Mother consults our General Malpractitioner.

me, which is what she got: somatically challenged, nipped in the bud, easier to torment, presenting simple sado-challenges. Exercising choice, she preemptively semi-unbegat me.

These embryocides don't require submersion to thrive. Gussied up and prettified as a purple flower bloom, they can follow you into existence and stalk you down the sidewalk with retro-abortifacient motives, like undercover Priestcrafty assassins shadowing your dad through the Relict Amalekites' home-sand—especially if you have weakened your immune system with incessant maestrobation and have left yourself wide open to invasion by such pathogens as engender the Sneeze Catastrophic.

This, of course, is assuming I'm not the result of parthenogenesis. Was I reproduced asexually as an outgrowth, a warty excrescence on the mommish superficies, or maybe mashed amongst her innards?

What if the person soon to be taken for

the kind of aborto-virus
that turns the river bile-yellow

"Dad" rode off immediately after meeting Mom? If he sneaked off with the odd-toed ungulate that was destined to be his true life companion before bothering to blastulize that month's Equestrienne Princess—and if Little Sissy is a trans-species facial-fornicatory bastardette, as Dad has always suspected—well, that begs the question of where the narrator of this Family Romance came from.

vii.

Sissy knows her papa's true whereabouts, and they are cis-Judeuphratic, and she goes into conniptions if her relatives try to suggest otherwise.

She has been in lust with him ever since coming close enough to his tickle-gizzard to be blastulated by it (assuming she's not the bastardette he suspects her of being), and she refuses to believe he's a turncoat rider for the Relict Amalekites, or even an agent provocateur pricking flanks on behalf of the Divine Krystelle Rex. The only correct data her ruined consciousness has been able to assimilate regarding the current male-parental situation is that her beloved "papa" is gone, and that he abides among strange beings.

bound in a backyard bunker

In going away to defy our condescendingly paternalistic Sovereign Ecclesiarchy, Dad left a condescendingly paternalistic void, which the youngest member of our attenuated clan can only supply with denial and delusion. She can't accept that her scrote-slinging heart-throb has been legally labeled such a monster that our own Grand

Religiopath will personally execute him if he ever comes home for her birthday. So she projects the monstrosity instead upon a weak-chinned gaggle of backyard squatters.

She whispers to me, in terror, late at night, the news that her "papa" has been taken hostage by the intruders whom she has visualized so horrifically and inaccurately. Dad has not really traversed a body of water, but has merely gone out of doors (which she is afraid to do) and is bound in a bunker sunken deep among the alien turds. He is about to be viddy-headed any minute, our Dad—rather, my poor siblette's *papa*.

"Want to know the saddest thing about it?" she used to weep, after dark, when the third occupant of our Gehenna appeared to be dormant. "Papa's handsome ride-loving glutei haven't glommed a saddle, but only the mud floor of a sub-excrement cell, the whole time he's been—" The pathetic child would shudder at her next word. "—*outside*!"

Of course, my half of our mutual dream-cloning of the paterfamilias is influenced by his letters home, for I retain the ability to read. And, in any case, there is only a limited extent to which our shared dada-dreams can coincide, due to our almost opposite physical natures. I, being non-girlish, am expected to cherish a more-or-less heroic Dadotype, regardless of how it turns my stomach at times. Sissy, on the other hand, being unambiguously non-boyish, is saturated with estro-gonado-corticoids, and therefore expresses her hallucinated anxiety for a Papa who needs motherly cuddles, thus:

"He's a hostage in a backyard oubliette, posing for naked photos and taking neon tubes up the sigmoid flexure! He is up to his powerful washboard pecs in dungeon drainage, fellow decapitees' spinal sauce!"

She passes out completely when Dad looks up through the grating, smiles and says, "Just like me, sweetie—

*Crusty ol' Doc Clyster has declared
Sissy's own spinal sauce to be problematic enough.*

waiting

you're waiting to die

No wonder she is obdurate in imagining our foreign guests as more horrible than ridiculous. She can have no idea how right she is about the, so to speak, earthy intimacy between him and, if not the squatters themselves, then certain of their further-off, less fortunate cousins.

viii.

Where did such a peculiar pair of siblings really come from? Do they necessarily share both parents? For all her protestations of pathogenophobia, it seems likely that Mom, at least once, allowed a certain differentially configured center of consciousness to mount her, to fasten onto her head, the Sneeze Catastrophic not only be damned, but courted, seduced.

I never saw her in her Equestrienne Princess morphosis, because she fleshed out immediately after I crawled like a worm-fish with newish leg sprouts from the mire inside her. But Dad insinuates in his letters that she formerly liked to sexualize more than the normally engaged organs and connective tissues, and to get herself blastulized by, shall we say, other than mainstream cooperators.

Literate avians, for example.

I wonder, and shudder, if that is where my own bookish bent originates, for I am a fan of the famous Bishopric Prize-Winning ficto-homilist, Blurt Vomitgut.

I believe this indiscriminateness is where the seeds, or spores, of her later pathogen anxiety were planted. She projects hypochondria upon us not so much as shame, or maybe just embarrassment. In the same manner will an alternative fornicator fret about T-cell count till he gives himself hydraulic apoplexy, his immune system meanwhile remaining pristine as the driven snow.

Pre self-imposed-exilic Dad was heard to speculate that Sissy might be the product of such a

One's true Darwinistic papa?

one-night facialization, "a loogy bastardette partial throat abort," as he sporkerized it.

Crusty ol' Doc Clyster, our Diocesan-Trained Familopath, is too professionally discreet to venture an opinion on the legitimacy of Daddy's ostensible seedlet, his little compulsive maestrobatrix. But the physician calculates that her pre-paternal-desertion Intelligence Quotient must have been so emphatically through the roof as to be "coated in avian excreta." I'll assume that's the sort of figure of speech employed by comic relief, and not a hint as to her biological sire's speciation.

But no level of bastardy can adequately explain the subject's present state of, as it were, "mind." So, what trauma caused her to doff her off-the-shoulder love-sarong, thick in fiber, and revert to pinafores and big-eyed mini-effigies and ghastly baby self-talk?

I'm told it's the norm for immature mammaloids to gambol. But I can tell you the giggles emanating from pre-adult members of the

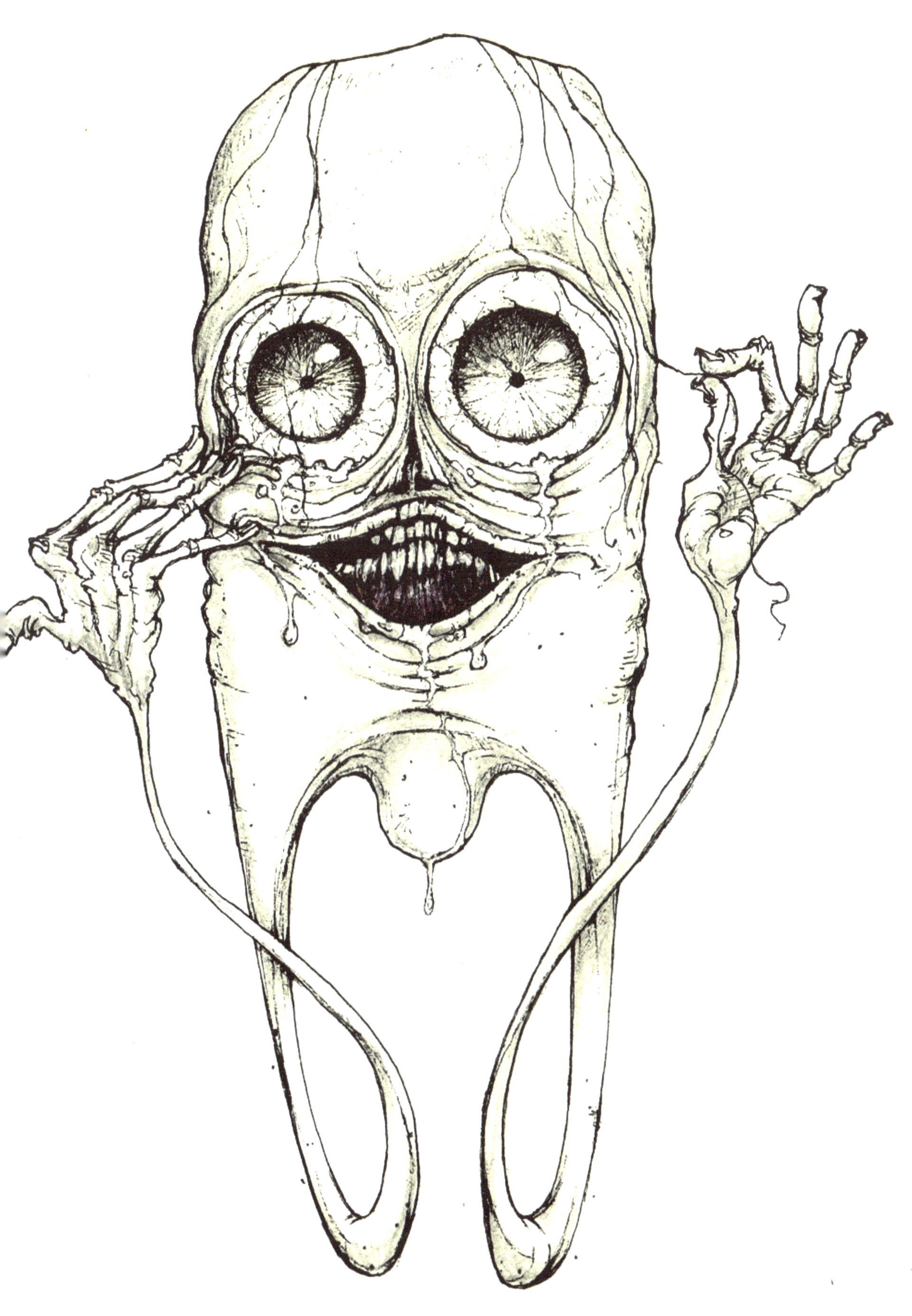

loogy bastardette partial throat abort

*Sissy touches her dolly-wolly just as
the Highest of High Physio-Functionaries
touched her.*

Endogamous Bellicose Caste are the most offputting noises outside a bonobo's asshole. Our playpen giggles sound like an emery board wiped against the whirling blades of a deep-fried toadstool shop's back alley exhaust fan. The sight of one of us skipping around the food table toting telesma-toys is emetic. We're an Amniobaptismo-Certified Regimental Ménage down to our alleles, and are meant to kill and explode things, not frisk and frolic. When one of us backslides to the youngster-sickness in adulthood, it could almost be considered a toxic medical waste disposal problem.

What trauma induced Sissy to revert? What caused her to shed so much of the high, elaborate, lovely coiffure Mom purchased for her head, the better for unwellness vectors to perch and nest? Why did my siblette go for the top-knot and pigtail effect?

Blame is to be laid at the spandexed feet of the matched set of Municipal Priestcrafters who, with great officiousness, made a house call in tow of their horrendous boss, long ago, coincidentally around the time of the paternal defection.

If Dad had slipped too far away to be disemboweled and righteously throttled therewith, the Grand Religiopath and his assistants could gratify their holy urges by performing a not entirely dissimilar disservice to the soft tissues inside his younger offspring's pelvis and head, thus teaching the unallegiant god-scoffer's brood a lesson.

So our domicile was graced with the presence of those distinguished types of personages who've abided a spell in the seminary/barracks and have been decorated with the zippered codpiece and other sacerdotal vestments and paraphernalia. They generally prefer inquiring into the more frankly penised youth of the State Confession. But in the present case they made an exception, and consented to accept her as a catechist, and to benedictate her.

They were supplicated to perform an intrusive yet exploratory inquisition into my little

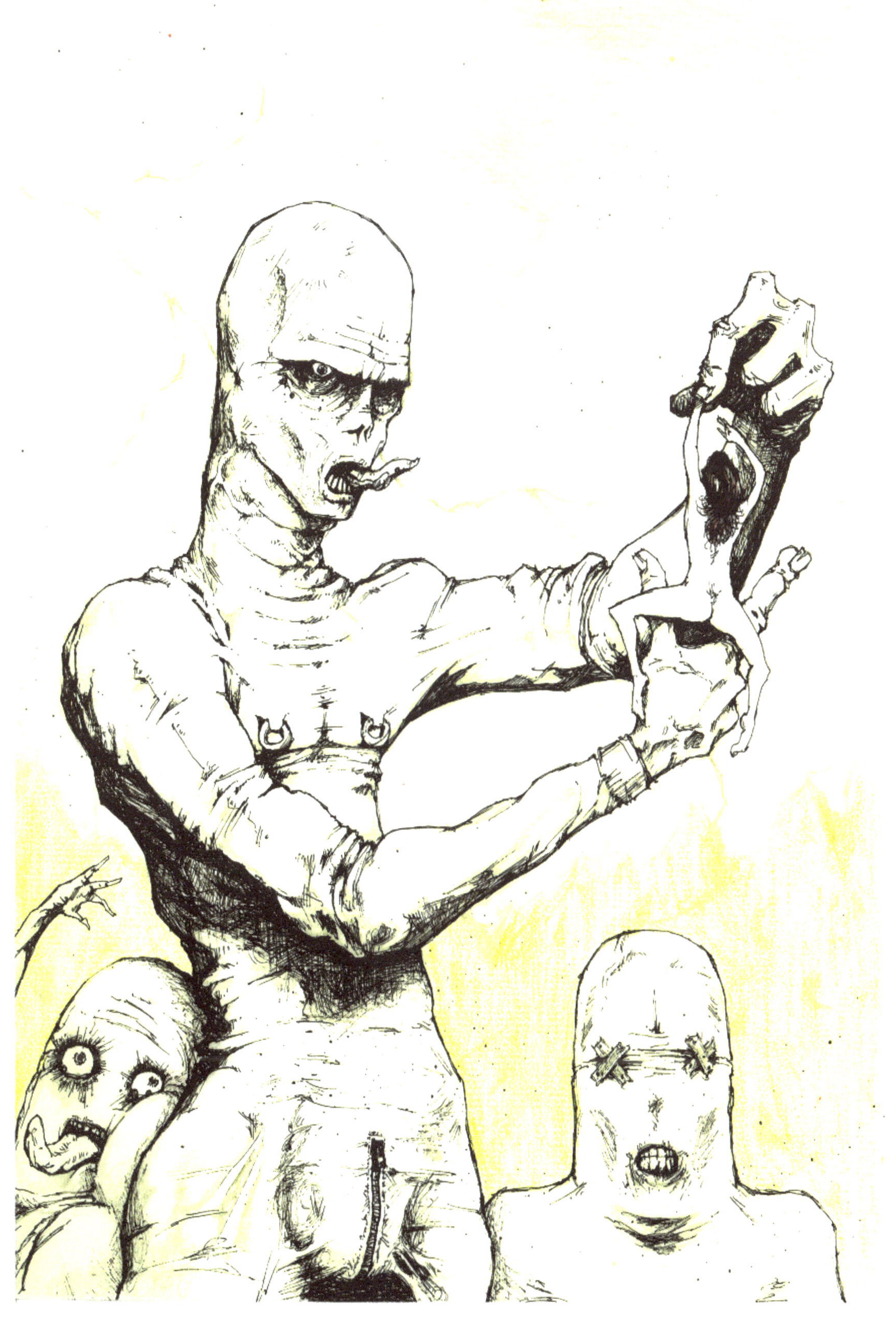

The Grand Religiopath improvises
a cunnilingual refinement
on the dread civil/sacral strappado.

sister's nether-soul, in search of elementary spirits that wanted casting out, or *exvagination*, to use the canonically approved argotism. They tried her via the dread civil/sacral strappado with a cunnilingual refinement, an innovation specially extemporized on the spot by the Highest of High Physio-Functionaries himself, a rare honor.

They wrung Dad's only daughter dry of self-possession, then left her spasming in the worst possible custodial care: namely, Mom, who makes the entire bureau of clergy-brutes look like lay-civilian hobbyists in the brain-reaming department.

*The refined civil/sacral strappado
was tried on Mom—once.*

ix.

Therefore, I do feel terrible leaving the child alone in the dining room with our tormentor thrice daily. But mine is a temporary abandonment, and necessary to our physical survival—in more ways than one.

Aside from supplying boluses and chymes for the perpetuation of our respective peristalses, my forays serve an emotional purpose: a release of red steam, a postponement the sort of love explosion that ends with one romantically familistic type metabolizing another, leaving little more than shrapnels of connective tissue on the dining room rug like vaguely decipherable red runes. This object in your hands may very well detonate with something scrawled and stomped.

Such a horrendous climax could be put off indefinitely, or at least postponed till it wouldn't appear premature, if I only had an emotional outlet. Say, an affectionate pet to commiserate with, to whom I could condescend without sarcasm, whose mind hasn't been poisoned against the likes of me.

During the relatively halcyon years before worldly war brought outlanders flocking into the backyard, we begged long and hard to be bought a lower being of one configuration or another, for us to love under the dining room window (hoping against hope that, if Mom agreed, she wouldn't immediately faciate with it and blastulate us a sibling with envenomed gills or something).

Sissy whinged as follows (this was before she surrendered most of her frontal lobularity and lip flexibility to practitioners of clerical crafts): "A lovely pet might suck into its own sinuses a few of

the vectors of unwellness that are so intent on catastrophically sneezing the vitality out of us."

one metabolizing another

Mom just hissed a haughty reply: "Minors
should be content to have their faces licked and

their thighs dry-humped by the vermin that already come with the house."

But then the interlopers came influxing, those ornitho-plantigrade viviparoids (more or less), who fill my sister's head with such horrible, if humorously inaccurate, images of themselves. Their arrival forced our stay-at-home parent to reconsider her decision regarding a guard pet.

Was it in order to alleviate her daughter's horror of the delusion-exacerbated bugaboos that Mom decided to procure a more or less bestial deterrent for their approach to our dining room window? What do you think?

Here's a hint: *of course not.*

Our materfamilias cherished personal reasons for changing her mind. And they were less motherly than geopolitical, less geopolitical than hygienic.

She'll protest dietary solidarity with our Sovereign Ecclesiarchy's "tragic victims" before each meal. She'll forego fructo-sorbets and condemn

Theretofore we'd only been permitted pretend fauna, such as this telesma-toy typical of Endogamous Bellicose Caste kids.

the kind of vermin that already come with the house

her brood to a lethally jejune diet on their behalf. But Mom's too infection-minded to sit still while their brethren pile, shall we say, self-evidence hip-deep behind our house.

Yes, perhaps you will not be surprised to hear that our visitors happen to be none other than displaced Relict Amalekites. These are the very wretches on behalf of whose stuck-at-home cousins we've become monophages, whose cries of Flamma-Mannified agony Mom claims telepathically to hear, all the way from the trans-Judeuphrates.

Our postal zone has experienced an irruption of these Middlingly Oriental war refugeniks. Our foreign policy of Conversion by Redundant Defoliant has come home to roost and molt. And squat and shit.

* * * *

They feel free hobo-jungling on our property because of what they presume to be our politics.

But, little do they know, the missing Cock of this Roost harbors motives of his own for taking part in the hopeless resistance against the biocide and occupation of their native envirulence. And it's not in the name of their liberation that Dad has given himself whole-body terminal saddle sores.

whole-body saddle-sores

It turns out Sissy was righter than she could have known about them. In her paranoia she accurately surmised their ethnicity/species, probably before you did. But their politics are a matter of indifference to her. All she knows is that Papa is gone, and a "big bad bishop-prick" cunni-boarded her for it. And, as far as she is concerned, these displaced bogeys are holding him, bound in a back-yard bunker, under a pile of their gratuitous turds.

surgical Flamma-Manna on-the-ground applicator for those hard-to-reach nooks of biology

Still musty behind the ears (assuming they grow ears), these autochthonous and immemorial natives of the Middling Orient, are heli-dumped into our laps as ever broader swaths of their tragically war-torn region are rendered uninhabitable and, of course, subsequently occupied by us.

not our most intelligent

How do the Municipal Priestcrafters persuade our homegrown melano-youth, the self-styled "Talibangers," to leave off their loiters and lurks along the sludgy linoleum of the Riparian Megalopolis' blight mall, to put on boots, fix bayonets on their Diocesan-issue pistols and wade across for a tour of sizzling and blistering on Flamma-Mannaed turf—rather, grit—which is so poisonous that its sting can be felt through a span of neoprene? Well, let's just say (speaking frankly) that the occupation of the trans-Judeuphrates is not exactly being carried out by our most intelligent baptizens.

In a secret letter home, Dad has supplied further elucidation—

In a disingenuous display of faux-group guilt, our—rather, your *"Sovereign Ecclesiarchy"—welcomes a tiny trickle of these wretches in without bothering them to master the local parlance, nor asking them to modify their quaint native rind. Witness, for example, their offputting shoulder dentition, and so forth. The obvious ulterior motive of such noblesse oblige is the conversion of these heathens to slavering Kryssie-pootums' One True Creed. Good Luck.*

The Relict Amalekites themselves, valuing their timeless heritage less than I do, want nothing to do with biocidal agents, and even less with idiotically incursive soldiery. One might almost guess they'd grown tired of the desert long before this, judging from the eagerness with which they come to you in search of "a better way of life"—which, from the sound of it, comprises the steadfast production of bowel movements on the baptizenry's lawns.

I hesitate to offend political sensibilities, if any remain in this time of worldly war. But it becomes necessary at this point to discuss—

the refugeniks' impersonal hygiene

—as it pertains to the very survival of the family that modifies this romance, and in particular to Mom's acquiescence to our weeping pleas for a pet.

Having been nomads since the dawn of sensical history, and having enjoyed till recently a broad range upon which to deposit their turds, our outlander friends are like bonobos who, despite relatively large cephalic indices, must never be allowed to go undiapered in a domesticated context because, in the wild, all they had to do was hang their elaborate nether-vents off the residential bough and swirl out bogs. Our roofless lodgers can never be persuaded to ease nature in a single circumscribed quadrant of the backyard—an advanced bit of calculus which even the average cyno-pet has no difficulty mastering. It would make my foraging chore easier, if not less unappetizing.

Tiptoeing has become the rule of the day for me as I gather our familistic calories from amongst the alien feculence. And, as if to endorse the Darwino-heresy, our visiting fecundators themselves seem adapted peculiarly well for tiptoeing, as they lurch about on downright struthious gams.

squatters in more than one sense

With such legs, feathers and talons, it's no wonder they got along so well with the first pet we persuaded Mom to acquire.

X.

Here's a notion of how deep Mom's politicization flows. For her, the outbreak of worldly war and geno-biocide necessitated nothing more or less drastic than the purchase of a faunal organism.

She got us the sort of under-being that comes recommended for a fundamental social unit of our socioeconomic level—namely non-mammaloid. Her only stipulation was that it should possess beak and talons sufficiently repugnant to discourage the approaches of foreign anuses to our dining room window.

Like its cousins, the sparrows, who camp-follow and settle on odd-toed ungulate droppings behind mounted units the world over, our first pet (her name was Winfrey) fed off shit. It was only natural behavior, and to be expected. The creature therefore quietly elected to be a failure, and to keep no spies away from the gaping aperture on the side of our house, as they were living snack machines.

In fact, the Relict Amalekites suborned Winfrey with their fragrant productions—but not the nutritious coprophytes that sprang so luxuriantly therefrom. Those Winfrey beaked fastidiously forth, coated with bilious saliva till unpalatable to any self-respecting upper-mammaloid, and spat out to rot in the grass.

So not only did the bird-brain demur from protecting our privacy, but she deprived us of easeful access to our sole source of calories—for we are myco- as well as monophages.

Our caste feeds off fungi sprung from feces. Did I forget to mention that? Cavalry meals

if only I had an affectionate being,
named Winfrey, to love...

must consist of spoor-borne, spore-spewing tid-bits: specifically the gills and pilei, the annuli, not to mention the volvae and stipes, of the Flyblown Fruiting Body, such as lately are being tumored so redundantly from refugeniks' dung. The intestinal congestion expelled by our visitants turns out to be an ideal incubator, lush and fecund as agar-agar slopped in a pyrex petri plate where fake neonates are coerced to sprout.

And what crawls with more pathogens than the former contents of beastly innards? You begin to see how inspired is Mom's choice of emotional control mechanisms. Shall I begin to enumerate the bushel-basketloads our dear maniac of a mater urg-es upon us? Between the two of us, my tiny, frail, emaciated siblette and I consume more superterra-nean budget truffles per day than flourish in a year on the Augean floor of a poorly janitored bovine diarrhea ward.

Sometimes I wonder what our dad would say if he knew this about the wretches whose

pathogenic supper guest

home-sand he is trying so sacrilegiously (if perhaps a tad sarcastically) to liberate: their repatriation would deprive his estranged brood of caloric intake. Talk about a conflict of interest—assuming Dad's interested enough in us to be conflicted.

xii.

Mom was sold on pietism as a parenting tool when Sissy ran afoul of the Grand Religiopath. She couldn't help but notice how thoroughly he and his pair of clerical sidekicks ream-jobbed the poor child's rational capacity.

When the outbreak of transriverine hostilities spirited Mom's hubby away from her affections and alienated his loyalty from our Inseparable Church-State, she decided that prayerific overtones should be morbidly slathered upon all food and other oral intakes until such time as her sole unambiguously male propinquity's triumphal return, even if it be in a zipper-bag (which, I suspect, would have been the preferred means of transport).

Plus, all the mumbo-jumbo over the food table had the added advantage of making this effectively war-widowed womb-wielder appear, to any ostensible peek-a-booers, to be a singularly parental type seeking solace for her pitiful semi-orphans in religification: a figure of pathos, as perceived by such rudimentary organs of discernment as might ooze and writhe within the sundry orifices pocking the knobs which so shoddily serve the Relict Amalekites as "heads."

When her husband mobilized off in brazen defiance of our Sovereign Ecclesiarchy, Mom decided to go all Mycosophical on us. Of course, it was a great coincidental help that we were already strict 'shroom subsisters.

Being a natural economizer, like so many un-double parents, she decided to go the indigenous route, to save on props and costumes. She furtively mail-ordered a shamaness diploma,

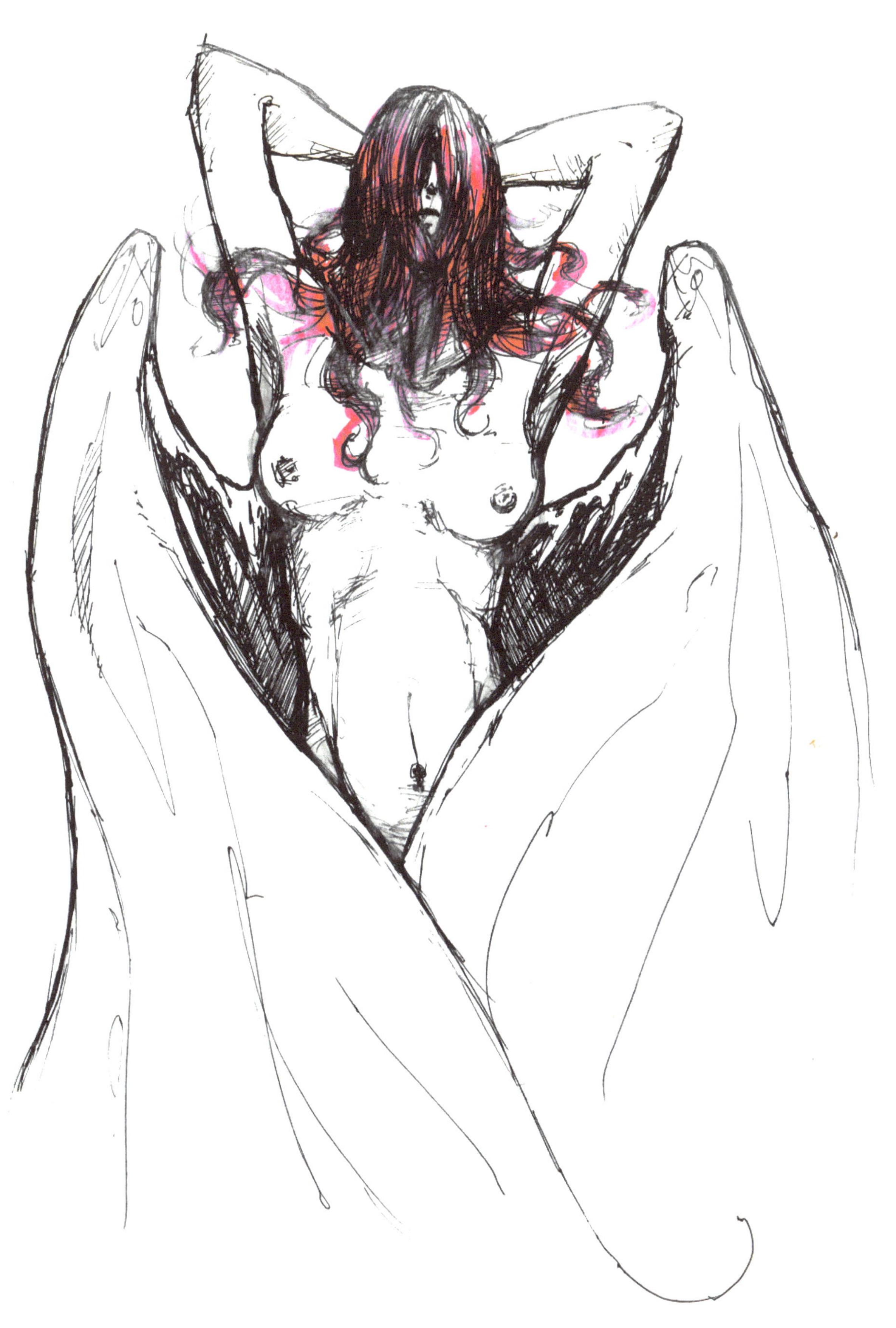

Mom's mealtime mumbo-jumbo

because, liturgically, it requires little more than nudity.

Thus she spared herself the expense of the pricey spandex gear of our Federal Sect's Clerisy. In any case she considers their zippered codpieces not only tasteless, but implicitly sexist in their gender-specificity. Besides, how can a minister primp and preen so, considering the pube-up nakedness Krystelle Rex displays in all splatter-iconic representations? Nudity is more congruent.

So here you have the true irony—no, absurdity—behind the Relict Amalekites being heli-shat upon our particular property with the ulterior motive of their proselytization. Their house mother forsook the orthodox ways of Krystelle Rex long ago to profess Mycosophy, a faith even more divergent from our national norm than their own uni-theism.

Having passed the novitiate in the mail-order seminary, Mom is obliged to consider all meals, indeed, all ingestions, sacramental. And she encourages between-devotional snacks.

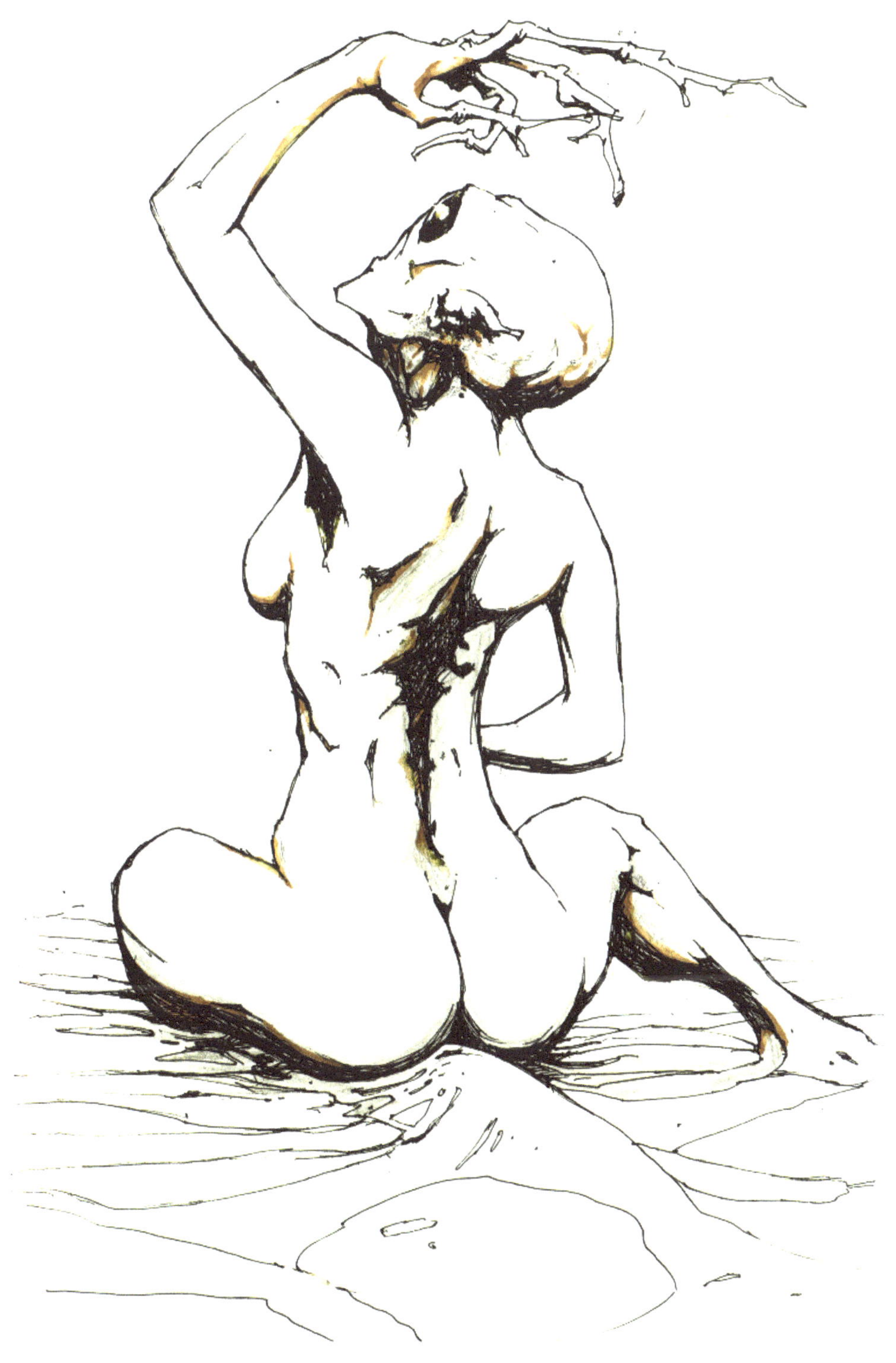

Nudity is more congruent for her.

Handfuls of non-sentient life forms that can be found in the backyard do the sacramental trick. There is no outlay for postage on eucharist wafers, because turdstools are the official holy food of her particular denomination. I guess you could call it transcultural symbiosis.

You've met the types, the ones who build an entire existence around 'shrooms. That, I fear, is us. This is a myco-mush subsisting Amniobaptismo-Certified Regimental Ménage. Citing the starveling Relict Amalekites (not the ones at the window, but their cousins across the ever-present waterway—who have more immediate concerns than peckishness, such as their bones emerging in the white phosphorus glow of Flamma-Manna), maniac Mater makes poor, problematically nourished Siblette and me eat our fungus beyond (and beneath) the point of it coming out our ears.

Not only Sissy, but even I hallucinate little naked men and women sprouting spontaneously from the Flyblown Fruiting Bodies. Mom calls them, too, "pathogens," of course, and reminds us that each mealtime is yet another reason to cover our faces with both hands when we feel a Sneeze Catastrophic coming on.

As for the flavor, well, Mom says, "It is solely in order to postpone etiolation that we swallow much of the matter which gets deposited in our oral cavities from time to time. Foodstuffs are not for titillating the senses."

It's almost suppertime. Hear Mom grunt from the meal prep nook:

"Wash u-u-u-u-u-up!"

* * * *

So, when Winfrey began scarfing up the fertilizing agent for our breakfast, lunch, dinner and, yes, eucharist, and potential caloric intake began to disappear from my foraging grounds, and our stomachs began to growl, Mom called in the Municipal

Winfrey spits out the good bits.

Priestcrafters to put our idiotically failed guard pet down.

The Grand Religiopath, who is no mycophile, came within half a pinfeather of a free poultry meal. He prefers to eat things live, slowly tongue-rasping them away, atom by atom, to prolong the agony and damnation. Sissy went comatose in anticipation of his house call.

Fortunately for Winfrey, before that Highest of High Physio-Functionaries could find time to drop by, a classic unwellness vector mounted her head, precisely because she'd been ignoring Mom's health warnings about ingesting excreta like some brutish sparrow. The poor beast wound up sneezing all her soft bodily tissues catastrophically away in aerosol form.

Sissy learned a lesson or two in virtuosic nasal bulemia pondering Winfrey's remains—out of which Mom improvised a fashionable boa. Pietistical hypocrite and vicious soul glutton though she be, our matriarch does have a certain fashion sense, for someone who dresses cheaply.

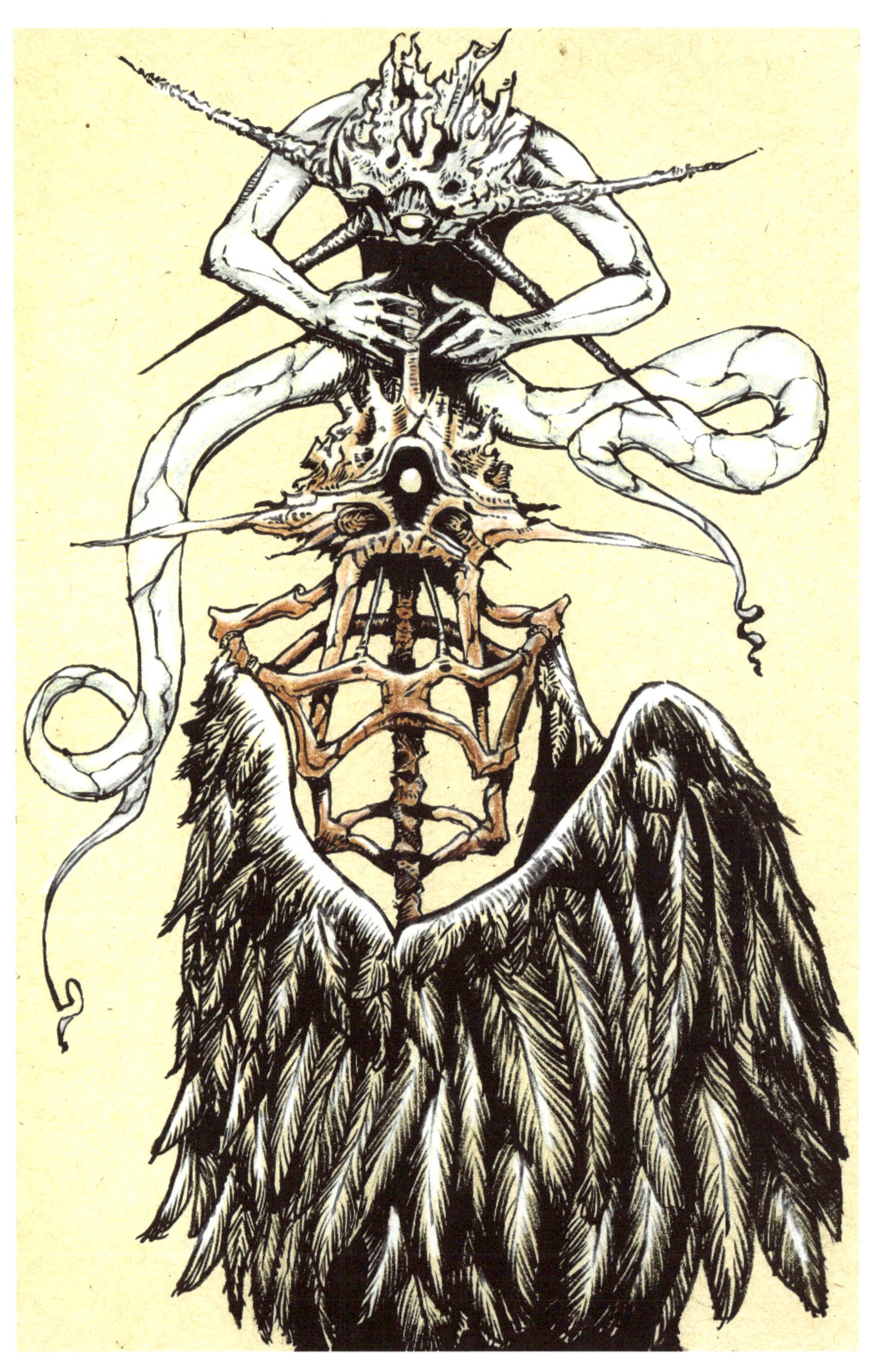

*Mom salvaged a fashonable
boa from Winfrey's remains.*

xiii.

If you could have seen how the latter personage behaved at the obsequies we improvised for Winfrey, you would understand why she wants neither eyes peeking at, nor ears hearkening to, our Family Romance.

Perhaps it's the hyper-religiose overtones Mom slathers upon them like some cloying giblet gravy, but even non-funereal mealtimes at our house take a strange effect on my thoughts and the inner pictures that accompany, or perhaps spur them.

Mealtimes take a strange effect.

In trying to steer through this uterine cyclone, I have had a rudder and compass. Under Dads' letters' influence, I've turned to literature. Deprived of an outlet for my unwholesome urges, I have come to know the books of the more or less almost great-ish ficto-homilist—

Blurt Vomitgut

—which were written deliberately on an infantile comprehension level in these latter days of childish literacy, thus depriving the author of full-grown adult self-expression, thus circumventing any writer's only reason for birth, thus leading, obviously, to suicide. This self-sacrifice on behalf of Blurt Vomitgut's retarded fans moved my Dad, who is, himself, tinctured deep in self-expungatory urges, like all full-blooded Endogamous Bellicose Casters.

Dad recommended Blurt Vomitgut to me as a Mom antidote and role model: "If your fingers are full of inked styli, you must drop that tickle-gizzard for a season or so. Plus, the Blurt-Man has a thing or two to say about homogametic progenitrices, having been nightmarishly suckled himself in times gone by."

Here's Mr. Vomitgut on that sore subject:

Orally gratifying religiosity, eucharistic pietism—the whole hyped-up scam of deicidal theophagy appeals to these so-called motherly types because it affords another, literal way for them to force their diseased will beyond our sinuses and extremities and directly, materially down into our guts. It's all we can do to roll our eyes broadly enough to make them self-conscious, to dissuade them from saying, "Take, eat, this is my body," as they sling those sacramental trenchers.

Uncanny, right? It's almost as if Mr. Vomitgut is describing my own situation.

*The ficto-homilist's pot boilers
are regurgitated in rapid succession,
if not simultaneously.*

Our remaining parent's nothing if not possessed of a highly developed sense of liturgical impropriety. In her ceremonious mode, such as she affects at those family dysfunctions called *equestriexequies*, Mom flits and flaps around labially. She suits up like a regular ordained vestal of the Grand Religiopath himself, and grabs the Ancestral Riding Crop in both hands.

At such times her torso assumes such an approximately erotic air, it's almost possible to ignore the giant hump that erupts from the dorsal area of all more or less healthy Equestriennes when in thanato-estrus.

Unlike certain other heritable confessions, our baptizenship passes with indifference, matrilateral or im-. And you can tell this Default Mitochondriac of ours is full-blood equite, eldest foal to boot, by the way her sire rides posthumously on her back. This accords with the mytho-bio-ethic of our caste: the Cavalryperson saddles up as a youth, dismounts at maturity, and remounts after death

It's almost possible to ignore her doubly prehensile hump.

upon the rightful heir, in the form of a doubly prehensile hump of greater or lesser substantiality, a semi-incarnation, only intermittently material, depending on hormonal and/or geopolitical circumstances. Mom must have usurped the primogenitalia, because, from sacroiliac to nape, she bears this auric embodiment of the agnatic nature, like a somatic patronym.

It's a semi-metensomatotic piggyback ride, which is unlikely to skip the present generation. And my dread is that she will try to wrap her thighs around my shoulders someday, before the time is ripe, when those thighs still course with the blood that makes her so pathological, before that red gravy has had a chance to sublimate into the quintessence of spirit. Like the odd-toed ungulates we all are under the skin, she might jump the starter pistol in this terminal derby. Then who will be the outgrowth or warty excrescence on the superficies of whom?

My dread is that Mom will jump the gun.

The current house- and backyard-bound cohort, regressively bred to ineffectuality, has slipped into decadence. Sissy would lose bladder control if ever brought into the presence of an odd-toed ungulate, or even an even-toed one. And I intend never to travel beyond our property, and to struggle with no enemy more formidable than refugeniks.

xiv.

As these are not the sorts of secrets strangers should be voyeuring, Mom consented to the procurement of a proper attack-mammaloid, once we'd scraped most of Winfrey's catastrophically sneezed atoms off the wallpaper. When we redeemed this secondary creature from the Pastoral Pound, it seemed to come fully equipped with teeth plus fur, along with—or so I hoped—the quasi-pooch's placentally-poached capacity for at least aping the outward grimaces and twitches of affection. We named the weird bitch—

Hildegarde von Bingo

—and posted her conspicuously in the back-yard, the better to monitor our surreputation.

It is strange that Mom worried about our particular voyeurs, to the extent of kicking loose funds for a second pet. It's not as though the Relict Amalekites could dish dirt among minds capable of forming bad, or even good, opinions about us. Indiscretion presupposes the ability to transfer intelligibility, and these are foreigners, after all. They can't even talk, not in the proper sense of the term. Let's just say, for now, that they rely on nonverbal skills.

On the other hand, if my sister is to be believed, they—or, rather, her distorted version of them (unfeathered, more terrible than ridiculous)—do make some kind of noises with their upper respiratory tracts. Like Mom pretending to hear the long-distance shrieks of their stay-at-home cousins as the skin melts off their skeletons in lumpy streams of Flamma-Manna, Sissy auditorially hallucinates our squatters' bestial vocalizations out behind our domicile.

As if deliberately to exacerbate such imagined agony with a stab of actuality, these savages have adopted the dining room window as their favorite place of social resort. Just as before, on Winfrey's watch, they like to hover and amuse themselves by observing our Family Romance unfold as the older generation rapes the younger of self.

Meanwhile they play fetch with Winfrey's replacement, the very cyno-vigilator that is supposed to be barking them off. Hildegarde von Bingo was bought to lick *my* face and dry-hump *my* thigh, not the homologous segments of their "heads" and lower limbs. Loyalty to purchaser is one of the chief traits touted in the promotional material for this species of womb fugitive, but only till the warranty dries up and crusts over, which it must have already done. She loves the intruders more than she does me.

Sissy can hear her distorted versions of them.

They have managed to suborn our second familistic pet as handily as they did the first, poisoning her mind against me every bit as thoroughly as they did Winfrey's. But this time, for a change, the thirty pieces of silver did not fall out of their assholes. Not by way of oral gratification have the refugeniks larcenized our haired sentry's loyalties. Fecal snacks have not entered into the process of corruption, Hildegarde von Bingo being, anomalously enough for her kind, disinclined toward coprophagy.

Rather, the trick has been turned by schmoozing of an alexical sort that can almost be called borderline-linguistic, conveyed by what can only be termed visual cues, for they tend to liase by retina rather than auditory nerve. Their non-patois is uttered silently, by sign rather than phoneme—that is, if you are willing to call flipping the bird ninety-seven different ways chit-chat.

Paradoxically, this should be the one means of communication unavailable to a creature which suffers this miserable cur's particular handicap. She could not be less suited to respond to hand yammer and other sorts of oglable quips, as she's been rendered eyeless as her new masters are larynxless. Samson squinting through curly bangs in the Gaza Strip was no more myopic than our mammaloid.

This particular rapine is not Mom's doing, for a change. Pathogens have not caused our quadrupedal purchase to sneeze both peepers out. Nor has the sacred handiwork of the Municipal Priestcrafters obviated her optic nerves the same way they reamed Sissy's brain. Look toward our family wellness bringer, instead.

*Pathogens such as this are not the culprits
bringing blindness to our sentinel.*

XV.

Like all responsible baptizens, we intended to spay our faunoid upon its redemption from the Pastoral Pound when, avian love having failed, something minus a cloaca and plus an umbilicus seemed to be indicated, the type that wants neutering. But we made the mistake of hiring our Familopath to proceed with the intrusion.

Like many comic reliefs, crusty ol' Doc Clyster's ill-at-ease around wholesome beings. Hence his choice of professions and his willingness to spend time in our presence. It's narrowly rumored that his abstruse education in bodily things has cracked apart a subcranial window sash that is painted shut in most heads, a jagged aperture that opens into the secrets of the Family Romance, giving him access to rare wisdom, which, of course, has nauseated crusty ol' Doc Clyster on a terminal basis, because he knows things far too disgusting for us mere lay-ignoramuses to imagine. That's why people are willing to pay him so much money to keep his mouth shut, pouted under immobile flounder-folds of pudge, a perma-puffed rictus of revulsion.

He's got the Hippopleptic Oath tattooed on the very ventricles of his gore pump, except for the line about those pessary-thingies that get poked inside incarnation canals—otherwise he would have attracted no patronage from our household in the first place. He only made that exception in the case of our quondam-puerpera, because he likes intruding upon her on a clinical basis.

"It's an education in itself!" he assures me, with an upper-middle wink.

*He spends all day elbow-deep
in other people's mucous membranes.*

Of course, contact buzz from the Flyblown Fruiting Bodily potency stored in Mom's endo-metrio-sacs is what opened the peep-hole amongst Doc's forehead pleats in the first place. Some attach high spiritual significance to the cornea that seems to have wedged itself in that hole. I suspect it's just a zit into which an eye-spotty pathogen has decided to hibernate.

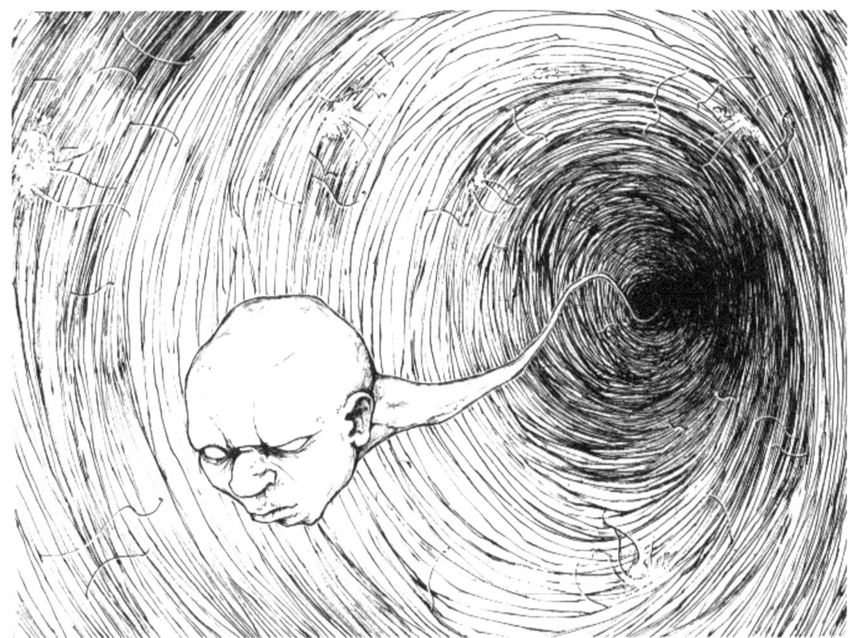

He likes intruding on a clinical basis.

They say his ersatz-third gawker enables him to effect miracles, such as commanding respect from society, even though he spends all day elbow-deep in other people's mucous membranes. The aroma of his right hand is so elaborately developed that it glows and stings the tear ducts; yet we must grovel at his three-toed slippers and salivate him "sensei" in the Nippo-manner. It's not fair.

As it turns out, ol' Doc Clyster is either hard of hearing or just possessed of an exceptionally chaste mind. In either case, with regard to our newly acquired attack-pet, the only word he heard Mom say was "balls," and he went after the pair above the waist. He scooped out the windows of Ms. von Bingo's soul rather than the sumps of her libido.

* * * *

So, three times per day I must make a few judicious throat-clearings as I sphincter myself

signifying just like a Talibanger.

through the dining room window, to forewarn our sightless Cerberus of my approach before I come to ground behind our house, where, in swirls of black mist, the unfaithful beast has been chained.

Before setting to work, I take a brief moment and attempt mutually to commiserate with her. But she mocks my advances and condescends to me instead of vice-versa.

How the accursed refugeniks managed to bring about this unnatural situation was a mystery at first. Even if she weren't minus the light it wouldn't have been easy. To measure the difficulties our guests encounter while trying to make sweet talk to a mammaloid, or to any other sentient being, I invite you simply to observe them passing idle time in our backyard.

Try to see them as they really are, unfiltered through my sister's schizoid corneas, and you will notice that, in posture and gesture, they bear a vague yet clearly forced resemblance to our own homegrown melano-youth, who creep along the pastel bubblegummy linoleum in our Riparian Megalopolis' blight mall: those stragglers among the halitotic Talibangers whom Municipal Priestcrafters have deemed unworthy to recruit for sizzling and blistering on trans-Judeuphratic sediment, who loiter, instead, along the superficies of disaffected sloth, and who, in their fundamental perversion, sport their love sarongs on the only place Krystelle Rex didn't wear his.

The first few times I faced our displaced intruders and tiptoed among their self-evidence, I wondered who had corrupted these poor Thirst World War victims. Where were they schooled to sign as glibly as any machine-pistol-packing rapist bred in the dioxin sludge of our Sovereign Ecclesiarchy's unconsecrated slums?

In outrage, I rhetorically demanded of Krystelle Rex to know what entity schooled my lawn-guests in the self-conscious posturing of the arms at lowland gorilla angles, in what might be called an act of kinesthetic reversion. What kapellmeister drilled them in such chironomous love croons as can woo the animalistic gore pump? Which agency persuaded the Relict Amalekites to "talk" with the same sort of sinister paw gyrations utilized

halitotic Gang-Talibanger, disaffected,
ethno-bred on the linoleum of a blight mall

by criminals to work out their sordid schemes? I cursed the insidious transnational seductiveness of our lumpen degenerate pop-sub culture, and how it can even turn the "heads" of wadi wallowers, on behalf of whose liberation Sissy lost her one and only lust object.

no longer safe for senior power-walking

But, in fact, my own class-ridden speciesism drew my suspicions too far afield. It turns out these wretches need attend no classes in Gesticulation as a Second Lingo. They are native speakers of their own special hand-yammer, natural-born experts at plying fingers like tongues, wrists like uvulae. (I mean in the unerotic way.) The phrase "natural-born" is here used in both the literal and synechdochic senses, as I learned from perusing the following ficto-homily by Blurt Vomitgut on the subject:

They have no muscular organs writhing on their oral floors, these erstwhile caravanners along the gummy grit of the Middling Orient. Nor have they any throats at all, much less the bitubular vocal tract that enables audible rap in upper mammaloid forms.

If I were susceptible to the Darwinizers' schismatic hissings, I might wonder if the somatic energy conserved by such otorhinolaryngologistic shortages was expressed, in the males, by their elaborate and tasteless mating crests. (I gag to speculate about the other two sexes.)

mating crest engorged
and metacarpals flexed for rapping

Perhaps this peculiar state of structural affairs has something deoxyribonucleically to do with the enriched choco-covered plutonium shells that our sophomorically misnomered "theocracy" has, with such sarcastic magnanimity, packed among squeaky styro-cashews and heli-crapped on them in Careless Packages ever since the promulgation of the genocide policy.

The refugeniks' default manual manner of "speech," so to speak, combined with certain impersonally hygienic customs different from our own (which I shudder to specify), has caused a cruel aphorism to gain worldwide currency. It has been aptly remarked that, in the Middling Orient (and now, in our backyard as well)—

All talk
is dirty talk.

The only question is how in the world they managed to whisper their uncleanly nothings into a deafened set of eye sockets. Was some false religio-magic involved? Did their peculiar trans-Judeuphratic god pull some prestidigitation? These questions may forever remain exotic mysteries.

Speaking of doing dirtiness with the hands, I suppose you've been wondering how long I was going to put off discussing—

xvi.

maestrobation

You search in vain
beneath your sheets for shame.
Best peek, instead,
at sheetrock overhead.
—Blurt Vomitgut

I learned, early and well, not to do it, no matter how
many aphrodisiacal Flyblown Fruiting Bodies I'm
urged to gorge in the loosely draped presence of

my beloved siblette. No matter how my bedroom wallpaper is swirling and metastasizing up to the ceiling. No matter how seamlessly Mom's quantities of fungus interblend the sensations in my soles with the tingles in the ridges of my scalp, and every me-bit in between, and regardless of the extent to which my bed sheets are behaving badly as barf in a bucket.

The Relict Amalekites make a big flap about being able to splotch the ceiling when they "chit-chat with Er's kid bro" (their wrist-down circumlocution)—as if they know what a ceiling is. Roofs were exotic enough among these manuring marauders even in the pre-Flamma Manna days, before we flattened every hovel up and down the far Judeuphrates bank.

Well they may brag, the savages. They don't have their female precursor suction-cupped overhead, vocalizing like a howler monkey, more distracting than any number of bugaboos nosing through the house-hole.

I believe Mom has no sense of personal boundaries.

The nightmare question is how she got the ceiling-splotching idea into her head as something that needed either to be forestalled or—horrible thought—participated in. For participation seems to be her intent, as she spreads and gapes up there.

Her sundry face-holes are multiple bull's-eyes for the initial squirts, which, at our house, it is decreed, must be triple. Mom controls even the staccato of our ejaculo-behaviors, our Sneezes Sub-Catastrophic. I believe she has no sense of personal boundaries. She cares little about follow-up garment splotches and post-nasal dewdrops—hence the camouflaging subtropical batik patterns on our infrequently dry-cleaned off-the-shoulder love sarongs, thick in fiber. She says dewdrops are Dad's department. I have no idea what she means by that. Something cynical, no doubt. I am, after all, half the rope in the tug-o'-war between her and the absent dropper of dew.

My unfortunate siblette, my notionless little sister, failed to master the negative skill of

Sissy must ignore the tickles
of the minor unwellness vectors.
In her condition she cannot afford a septal orgasm.

unself-disabuse, though much stricter means were employed in her case to curtail the ipsation. This is because, being unambiguously genitoried, her congenital lasciviousness surpasses mine.

The less said about her undeviations the better, so allow me to expatiate further upon them.

She once was such a looker. Even Mom seemed to notice. The pathogens she attracted were only the prettiest: petite, pale and ersatz-eyeless. In the name of pudency, Mom had always allowed both of us to raise our love-sarongs to off-the-shoulder levels, covering our sundry nipples; but in Sissy's case straps were added, as anchors, further modifying the Krystelle Rex look (which is to risk misdemeanor sacrilege). We didn't want anyone other than consecrated men of the spandex intruding upon the youngest member of our Amniobaptismo-Certified Regimental Ménage, on a clinical basis or off, before she reached the age of reasoning-with.

*the Seven-Course Achoo,
the Whole-Grain Gesundheit*

When she attained that liminal chronology of cajolery, Sissy entered the requisite post-pubescent rebellion phase. In her case it took the form of forsaking our ancestral monophagia and coming out, on the socio-nutrimentality front, as a reform Mahayano-Insectivore. Hence her unwillingness to take in proteins from sentient flutterers, with or without pseudo-eye spots, unless they happened to tumble down onto her lower lip of their own karmic klutziness. However, due to Punjabo-spiritualistic considerations hailing from way beyond Middlingly Anywhere I can imagine, all head-alighting unwellness vectors must be anesthetized by her halitotic rigmo before surrendering their exoskeletons to her prim incisors. Fads come far-flung these days.

"Our bastardette doesn't have an eating disorder," protested Mom. "She's just small-boned. How many Bruising Betties wouldn't give their left sirloin for such subcutaneous petiteness on the skeletomuscular level?"

In this malnourished child, the Sneeze Catastrophic has metastasized to bypass the epiglottis and engage the esophagus as well as the trachea, in the colloquial sense of the Seven-Course Achoo, the Whole-Grain Gesundheit, where one uses a serviette to blow one's nose, as in hemo-bulemia of the bitubular vocal tract.

So, what brought her to this crisis? Why, of course, the trauma was—

Crusty ol' Doc Clyster attempts to wean my sister off the ipsistic peccadildo.

maestrobation itself

—and the afterglowering post-trauma as well. She was caught "Rocking the boat," as polite society equivocates the way girls do it, which is apparently even rowdier than the methodology of their more or less non-girlish house mates.

When the Grand Religiopath and associates failed to cure her of such crassness, crusty ol' Doc Clyster, our trusty Familopath, was conjured. All clad in white, he appeared at her bedroom door like a phosphorescent toadstool, the albino kind that hickeys lightless cave walls.

"These self-starved coiffure-shedding femino-juvies," he observed before setting to work, "suffer from what are medicinally dismissed as *paternopenile issues*. The patient's pater being up to his penility in the Styx we all must wade eventually, I reckon she's pining away."

"She hasn't had her innie bred for an under-age," corroborated the next of skin.

Luckily, this time there was no way the three-eyed house-caller could, deliberately or not, misapply his orbit scoop, as the word "balls," remaining unuttered, was not misinterpreted.

xvii.

My dear, tiny, gullible, hopeful siblette's favorite bit of Dad-lore—indeed, the only myth she entertains as having an atom of factuality, apart from her self-concocted yarn of oubliette interment—is the one that claims he was a blasphemer even before crossing the Judeuphrates, that it took no demonically-induced crisis of faith to drive him to apostasize from the chainifixed and wormolated arms of the Divine Krystelle Rex.

No, Sissy believes that, when young, he was that rarity of rarities in an inseparably churchy and stately theocracy such as ours: a home-grown peacenik. If this is true, I can guarantee it was well before he got wowed by a certain Equestrienne Princess at the gala defense industry expo. Mom would disturb anyone's peace.

That's a qualification which our Family Romance's comic relief, crusty ol' Doc Clyster (who has, several times, been in a position to know whereof he joshes) is prepared to concede.

"Your dam could stampede a cadavalry cortège," the malpractitioner has been heard to quip.

According to this (let's speak frankly) ludicrous legend, bachelor pre-Pop was forcibly ridded of pacifism's civil abomination by the very same mob of clergy-brutes who later would not so much fail to cure as fail to cauterize his only daughter of maestrobation. He was shown, by means of the Grand Religiopath's lingual intrusiveness, the error of his passive ways. The same ordained organ which would one day cunnilingulate his younger offspring with the civil/sacral strappado penetrated his brain via the left auditory meatus.

It took no demonically inspired crisis of faith...

To this day, they say, my non-egg-bearing forebear wears on his person the stigma of his error like a scarlet letter transliterated phonetically from a paleo-syllabary. Talk about tattoo regret. Talk about trendy unblood-lust outpacing subcutaneous discolor.

It is murmured about the Riparian Megalopolis that the Grand Religiopath, having tongued literally thousands of sinful orifices, tasted something extraordinary in Dad's cerumen. And this Highest of High Physio-Functionaries, like a dog with its first smack of hemoglobin, still lives for the day he can find time off his busy schedule cunni-boarding baptizens' siblettes, personally to ford the Judeuphrates and finish the meal he started so long ago. If this is his plan, it will be a chase to remember—assuming he doesn't meet his mutual nemesis wading the other way. Our progenitor's due for a homecoming. Rather, *the* homecoming.

While I have no doubt the Grand Religiopath likes the smack of earwax (probably his own best

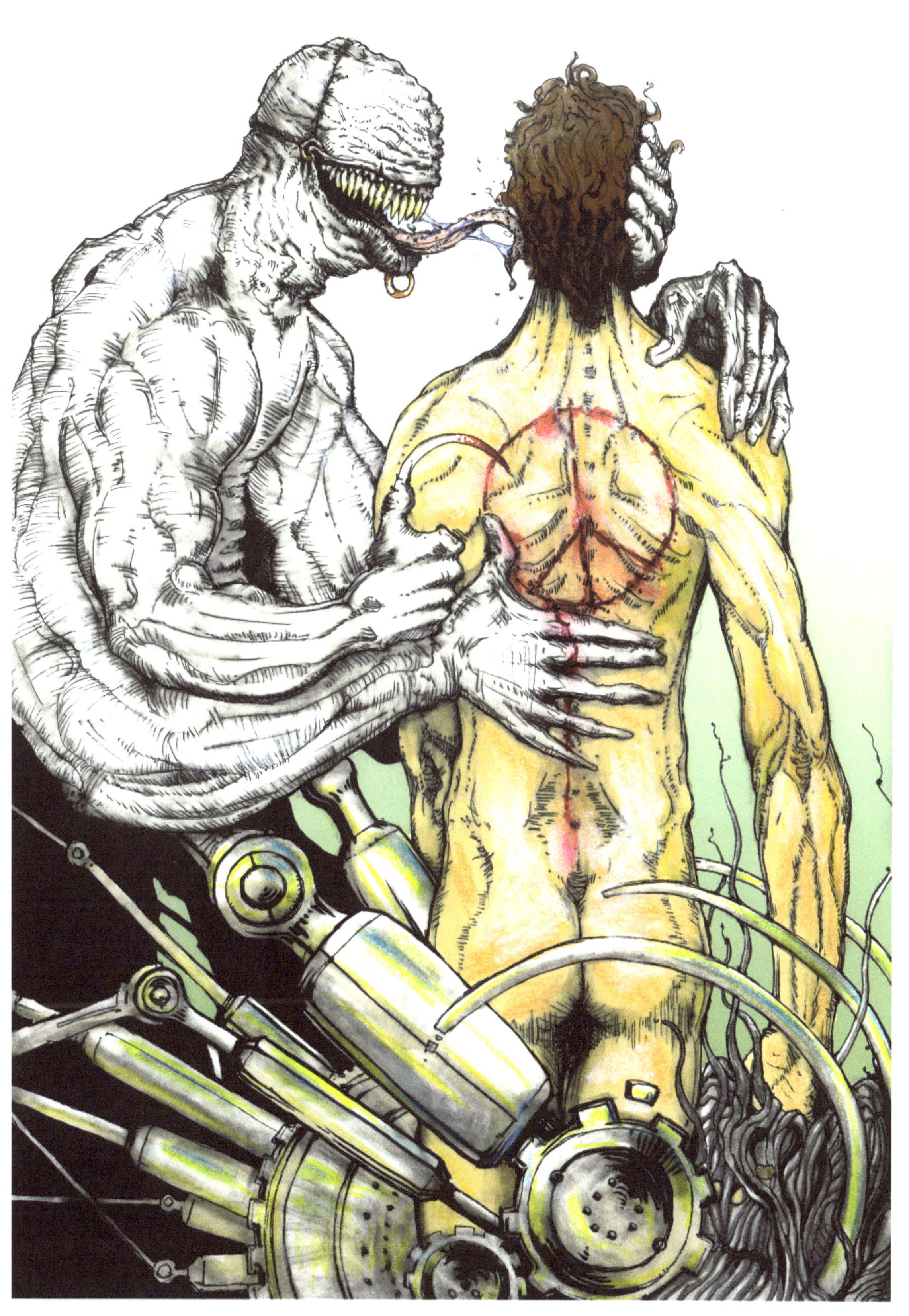

Dad is cured of peacenikism.

of all), I find my mental eye unable to maintain an image of any Endogamous Bellicose Caster, Cavalrous Subdivision, as peacenik. However, this is not to say I don't hold in common with my sibling a number of unreconstructed confabulations featuring her "papa."

Like most neurotically cloistered youngsters enslaved to a hypersexuated materfamiliarizer, Sissy and I share identical quasi-incestuous head visitations, without knowing which of us thought what part first, and whose sense organs were originally engaged, and via the insidious agency of which pathogen they were vectored between us. I'll presently cite one unwholesome co-daydream as an example.

The puissant scrotum-wielding figure who appears in most of our shared inner-skull projections prefers to keep his trouseredness ambiguous. Sissy can't bring herself completely to expose the patriarcho-schwanz for which she nurses such a damaged brain-suffusing letch. But it is plenty titillating for a congenitally lascivious daughter to imagine Papa sunken up to his upper pubis-line in a saline solution which hovers, in the temperature department, between balmy and clammy. "Amniotic" is an adjective that springs to mind.

This time it's not fetal me awash and grinning in the gritty lymph. Our father is fording, keeping the amniobaptismous serum at the same level down to which Krystelle Rex's tormentors rolled the sacred love-sarong.

And here's where our mutual infantile paramnesia gets fuzzy, or, rather, fluid: we recall a sluggish river. At least the ambient element reconstitutes itself in the back of our heads as vaguely fluvial. But I can't be sure. There is something odd about this accumulation of moisture.

I suspect the body of sauce to be materno-wombular, and ourselves to be scoping from that most proto- of POVs, the in-utero, from which reverse angle unwelcome strangers peer back at you via ultrasound scans. Therefore our parents must have sexuated while we were yet embellied, and we conjunctive preemies somehow remained unaborted by such an untimely fellaciation.

"If so," marvels Sissy at my bold suggestion, "Papa must have the muscliest, most upper-horned pecksniff in all counter-zoology!

His face remains strangely unseeable behind his tumescent mating/mayhem crest, and his general tenor remains anabolically steroidal, as though only a featureless mass of sinew and brawn could be imagined tangling fruitfully with such a gorgonerilla as eventually expelled us.

I say to my little sister, "Maybe our parent wades up to his washboard midriff due to scrotal shame. He's bracing himself for the embarrassing end which the Municipal Priestcrafters have planned for him: the rolling-down of his love-sarong to borderline frontal-nudist level."

You could with justification expect me to go off and search for him, in the usual Telemaccharine manner: the boilerplate Pa Quest undertaken

Mating/mayhem crest in full tumescence,
Dad wades, pubis-deep.

by a slim majority of unambiguously heterogametic youth. And you might also be canny enough to infer something idiosyncratic about my genetic makeup when I announce to you, here and now, that I intend to dog-ear nary recto nor verso of this romance poking around for anyone, least of all a Darwinistic parent, male, female or hermaphropoid.

Nor will I be required to.

* * * *

Horned as a desert patriarch, Dad negotiates the Judeuphrates. And if the latter comprises his uterine element, then the enemy cavalry must be his true vocation. Just as I was chased by Mom's embryocide, he is hounded by mercenaries—sorry, *contractors*.

He is being reconnoitered from a high cliff on this bank. The eyes that tongue him belong to The Grand Religiopath. Bolstered, underwired and

reconnoitering

propped in an exacerbated version of the spandex chasuble, the latter dignitary has finally found some time off his busy schedule, and the pair of them are about to meet, again.

xviii.

When the seasons change, the time rolls around for the Relict Amalekites' feathers to disattach from their pores and adhere to their turds, as though the latter were clots of tar smeared on a defrocked politician.

While foraging in metamorpho-molting season, I must shunt aside vast complications of plumes from our sustenance. I can't help but think of Father laying his presumably weary exile's head to rest on foreign sediment. And I wonder if his hosts' sheddings are downy enough to pillow his tongue-rasped sinistral eustachian tube.

Unfeathered, the refugeniks' offputting shoulder dentition and upper carapaces come into view. You'd think molting would make them look somewhat more mammaloid, but it has the opposite effect. One can only wonder why their designated demiurge made them like that, after giving them such an inefficient method of chit-chat.

The perplexity remains on the table: how did these inarticulate slouches, with their strictly visual means of communication, not only get through to, but win the allegiance of our retina-challenged attack-beast, she of the scooped orbits?

Every day, more than a couple of times, I ask myself that question while dropping down from the dining room windowsill and facing my supercilious, snooty cyno-pet. And a superstitious suspicion inevitably follows: that Hildegard von Bingo's mute seducers might have been endowed with something like cross-species telepathy by their particular idiosyncratic plasmator—

Chief Plasmator of the Trans-Judeuphratics

Jawhey
the Stylus God

—who wrote and, having written, relieved his botched creatures of that chore. That's why they employ dactylology and have no paper (a deficiency, as you shall see, with impersonally hygienic consequences). The blabbed solecism bears the onerous logos no less lightly than the scribbled.

The Relict Amalekites are the self-styled Originally Selected Beings of this particular hypostasization of celestiality, whom they reverence as the Unitary Executive and Decider of the Present Solar Clump.

He sounds to me like more of a brain lesion than a transcendent being; but nevertheless he has officially to be adored, also, by the heretical heart of our male parent who, at least technically, is a convert. Therefore, if he weren't just trying to be funny galloping under Jawhey's banner, Dad would be a denier of our very deoxyribodoxy.

Transcribed below is some of the differentially fonted promo material which undercover cells of espio-proselytizers attach to disutility poles late at night:

In the septafold naves of his cathedralic heart, Jawhey suppurates a special letch for his concocted creatures.

It is written that, with each Palmer-Methodical stroke of his chthonian biro, he stabs a time-louse on your life scalp, thus numbering your evanescence in this particular niggling Solar Clump.

Disinterest is his rule. The appearance of a mad cackle is only lent by an accident of connective tissue deployment.

Rumor maintains that the Relict Amalekites themselves flaunted such a physiognomy, in his image, before doing their equivalent of lapsing (which I'd rather not picture, if you don't mind).

an Ur-Self being torn apart

It appears as though this scribblesome fellow, too, like me, was only semi-aborted, early in this cosmic day, pinched between the raggedy hemorrhoids of the Big Emanation—or so his communicants (like, presumably, Dad) are schooled.

Some blasphemers insinuate that our Redeemer, our Mediator, our Savior and Advocate, the Divine Krystelle Rex, is nothing other than the sibloid of this Penultimate Penman, whose Orientally Middling demesne we presently seem to be holocauterizing. Some snicker that our pinch-slugger in this inning is just a modification of that earlier entity, the Stylus God's fraternal wombmate, yet nevertheless his immortally mortal antagonist. If this is accurate, our family exemplifies the split: Dad has gone over to the service of one imaginary figment while we continue to truckle under the sway of the other.

Some believe that the Thirst World War between our two regions is nothing less than an Ur-Self being torn apart, the macrocosmic soul depriving itself of integrity; that our field marshal is one and the same as theirs; that the influx of seeming aliens into our municipality is an attempt at physiopsychic individuation. It's a backyard family reunion, minus potato salad.

Dad propounds his own theory in his secret letters to me. He considers our tutelary C.E.O. (his, too, pre-apostasy/desertion) to be an effete version of the more arid deity, a wimpy, warty outgrowth. And, like all poor imitations, "Missy Kryssie" tends to overcompensate. "Her" pitiable chainifixed, wormolated condition demands the drafting of a warrior caste whose groin-strapped troopers are capable of waging industrialized biocide, while "she" serves them as a regimental substandard, threadbarely drooped on a hula hoop high over their spiked heads. Such a raggedy effigy requires a Grand Religiopath, staffed by a bureaucratically bloated corps of theocratic apparatchiks, who not only impose their etiolated godlette's will, but pull straight from their sacerdotal asses the very content of that will.

*The divine Krystelle Rex
tends to overcompensate.*

our propinquitoid kithkin,
our fetiform teratoma,
our homunculesque fetus in fetu

Meanwhile, Jawhey, the original version, the sire of You-Know-Whom Rex (surname pinned on with semi-conscious irony), presides singlehandedly over preliterate, almost prelingual Bedou-doofuses—none other than our very own osculating cousins, our kithkin—who don't even wear trousers, as far as anyone can ascertain (apart from their saddle-straddling soldiery, for Parthian reasons).

Our current incursion is therefore autoimmune. Our half-hatched seed, our asexually grunted excrescence, our fetiform teratoma, our homunculesque *fetus in fetu,* is impinging (like merely non-girlish me sphinctering out the dining room window) upon the territory of the rightfully autochthonous. Our ignorant armies stomp through the Stylus God's backyard like me tiptoeing among his displaced devotees' droppings.

Meanwhile our clergy-brutes slanderously demonize the Relict Amalekites in the manner of Little Sister hallucinating them pincered around the glazed introitus she fears to approach.

more, and less, to the divine Krystelle Rex
than meets the eye...

On several levels, then, it's a question of who in our Amniobaptismo-Certified Regimental Ménage forsook whom. If we are, as Dad insinuates in his letters to me, indeed the parasitic twins of his hosts, see how doubly deep the tragedy of Little Sissy's delusion sinks. She harbors these inaccurate images of her proper propinquitoids as different and dangerous, protean as they are delusory.

xix.

I am willing to entertain a certain grudging admiration for the big snaggle-puss in the transriverine sky. But it's difficult to credit him with endowing his cultists with cross-species telepathy. Worldly war and bio-genocide are middlingly important theodicy-twisters; but the real head-burner is this:

If it's not the telegnostic providence of Jawhey, then via what physiological contrivance have the refugeniks persuaded our sightless Cerberus not to be nice to me? Might the answer be found in that lowly means of perception sunk at the opposite extreme of the sensory spectrum from the sixth, the ethereal one? Conscious as we are of the Sneeze Catastrophic, should we be probing Hildegarde von Bingo's (let's speak frankly) over-extended snout?

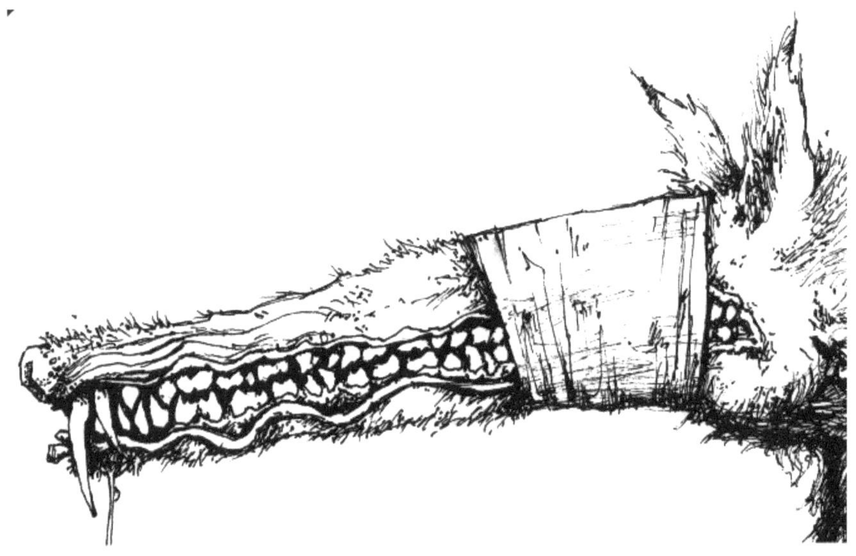

nasal nodes more than sufficient...

Confessors of the Crypto-Darwinizer heresy have been heard, in back alleys, to mutter under their halitosis about this very topic. They say that, boasting booger-tunnels somewhat lengthier than our own, this particular speciation of pettishness totes extra ranks and ranges of stench receptors, the kind that are left bare when we succumb to the Sneeze Catastrophic.

Like bat-sonar pinpointing a blood-succulent mosquito twenty feet away on a moonless night, these nasal nodes are more than sufficient to detect subtle yet lexical posturings of deaf-mute digits, provided the latter exude an idiosyncratic odor of their own.

Might, for some odd reason, the Relict Amalekites' grasping, scratching, maestrobating, chit-chattering organs carry some sort of aroma that appeals to natures even more brutish than theirs? How else could they capture the attention, much less the loyalty, of our familo-pet, blind as Lady Justice herself, and teach her to signify like a Talibanger? It's not for lack of comprehension that our on-special bargain-acquisition neglects to bark off the snickers hurled through the flung-open sash by the very entities against whom she was bred to protect me, her rightful master.

It remains a mystery from the more than Middlingly Mysterious Orient. As such, it's a cause for Mom to induce immune system anxiety in us.

Not surprisingly, she instructs me to steer clear of the followers of Jawhey, not due to their religio-politics, but simply because they hail from elsewhere and their hands probably smell weird in some way imperceptible to other than cyno-snouts.

The Other from Elsewhere plays host to unwellness vectors that can alight on you. Except when performing my nutritional chore, I should stay out of the backyard and remain in the dining room being raped of vitality by Mom, because these outlanders will cause differentially evolved pathogens to alight on me and make me do the *Disastrous Achoo* (as Dad calls it), and I might even pass the deathliness on to my little siblette.

differentially evolved outlander pathogen

XX.

So, have Mom and I instilled an obstressive-ex-pulsive fear of the Sneeze Catastrophic in you yet? Congratulations. Dry-heaving phobias temper the abs and make you more attractive when autopsy time rolls around.

Speaking of which, there is contagion on these pages. There's a flu to make the bubonic plague look like diaper rash, to make redundant defoliants feel like annealing balm for that rash. If I were a maniacal mater, I would have so many warnings for you at this late stage that you might hesitate to turn the recto, to peel back the lids on this gawker.

*obstressive-expulsive fear
of the Sneeze Catastrophic*

I would, for your own good, make you feel like a helpless, small creature fastened to an eyeball with a chain more adamantine than those which transfixed the Divine Krystelle Rex's elbows.

Depending on your level of soul-preparedness, this Family Romance could turn out to be like a spell in the most horrific of all torture chambers. The famous rat cage just might get muzzled to your kisser—except you're the rodent, and you've been hampered with a predisposition to rabies. And a membrane has metastasized along your proximal, intermediate and, yes, distal phalanges, where the vectors of unwellness have taken control and secreted sheet tumors.

But this does not mean you need fret about having picked up a pathogen and passing it on. You don't lack permission to commence considering this Family Romance with a sneeze. Go ahead and hurricane hard enough to blow back this page. Phlegm-paste it flat against the verso. Take a peek

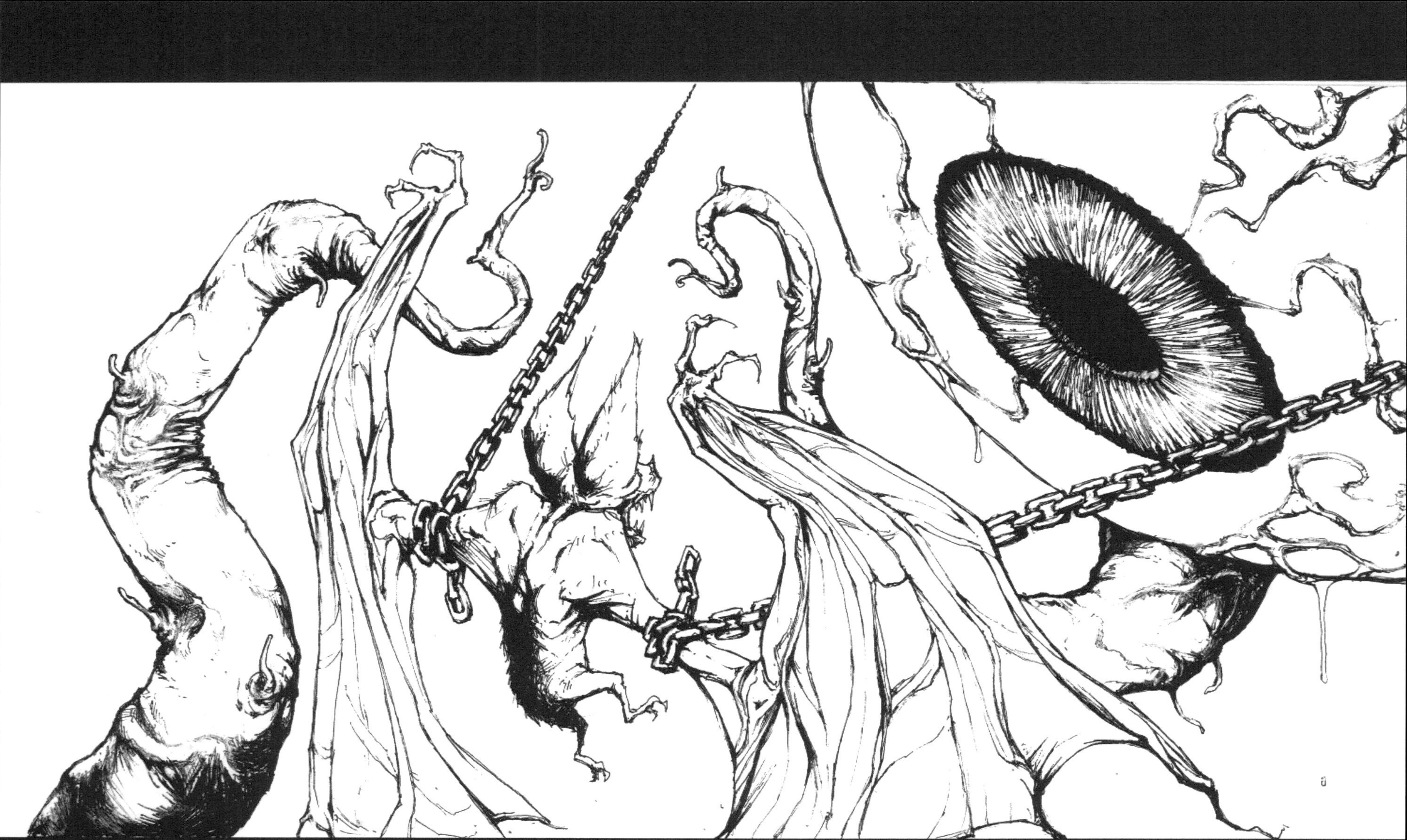

You're the rodent.

through the eyeballs you just atomized in a coarse red shpritz among the tantalizing tints

An eight- to twelve-hour proprio-spelunk is indicated at this point. You know, the kind you get sucked into after being sent to your room—not without, but, worse—*with* your dinner. And you've not been issued the usual personified tallow invigilator to distract the notional flooding that accompanies any unlit bedtime in such a household. It would amount to child abuse if you didn't get there first and prefix the *abuse* with *self-*.

But first, before moving any further into this proposition that is shuffled in so many layers between your fingers, it is recommended that you pause a moment and meld the stacked deck called yourself. There could be something far worse than a mere prettified Mom-bug mired in this cellulose sandwich. It could be waiting to be picked up, not by your sinuses or extremities, but by your immobile soul. An immaterial pathogen, so to speak.

When you've been persuaded to eucharize way too many mush-bowls, prepared by a not so much over-anxious as sadistic progenitrix, a hyper-religiose landlady-shamaness who tries to conceal her perfidy under a veneer of 'shroom piety—you often wind up mired in

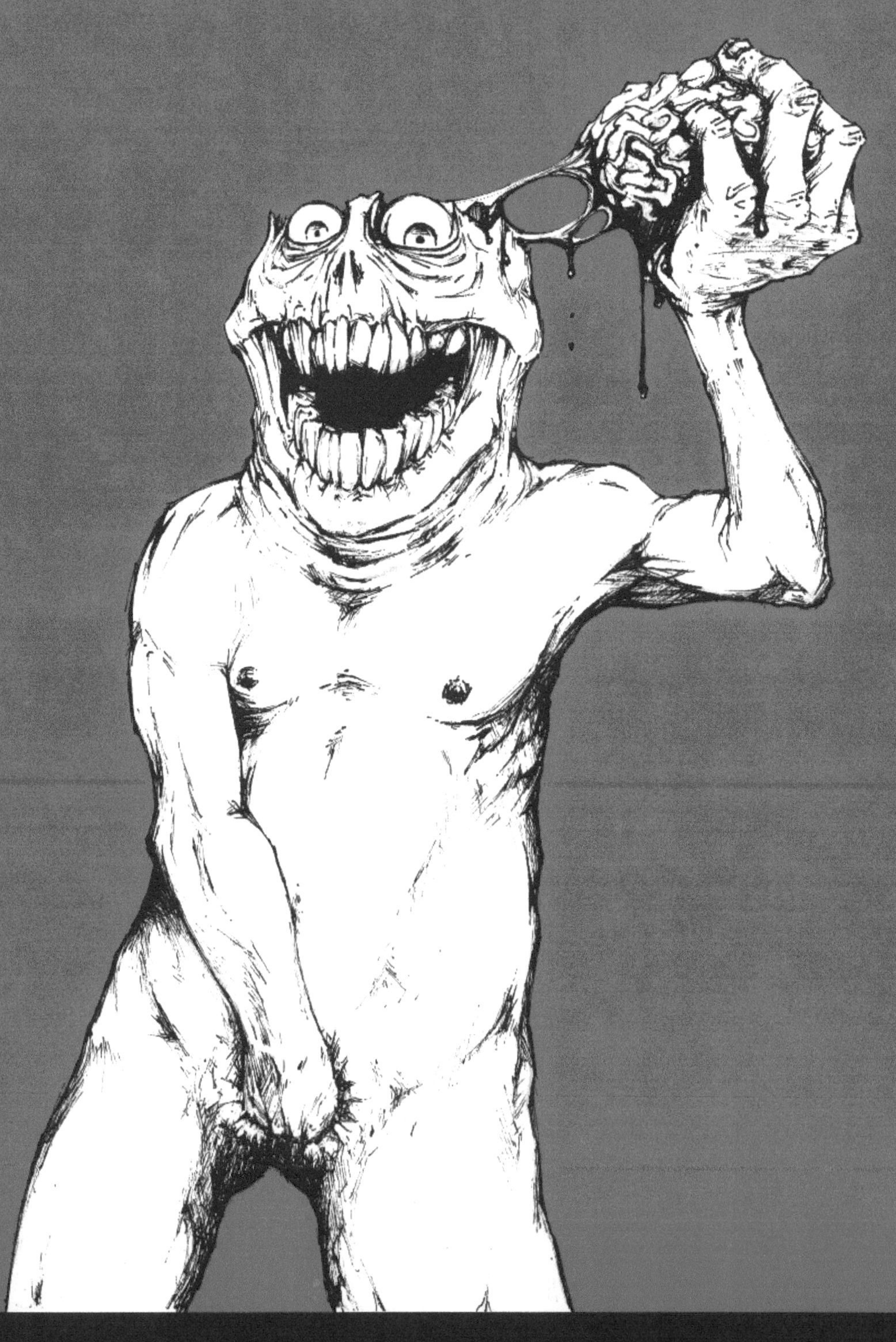

Prefix abuse *with* self-.

these hellish eight- to twelve-hour entheospections, hoverings of neuro-toxicity that make you understand why your melanin-challenged ancestors were traditional mycophobes, those moods that admit no border between what you see and what you'd give anything to unthink about what you can't bear to look at.

Such is the permanent post-prandial mood at our house—except inside Mom's own head, of course. Her inner pugnacity is such as to render the hugest, most crawling turd-growth into nothing more than a dandelion fluff against an eyelid. Her vitality dissolves us, embosoming entheogenicity itself, like vitriol buttering an unleavened wafer, and she's perma-cheery, eyes, mind and, especially, mouth wide open.

Are you ready for that? Stroke your head and think deep into the tentacled core of your subcranial colloids. Are you really prepared to attach your retinae so tightly to what you hold in your hands at this moment, until you think all the way down to—

the Relict Amalekites' impersonal hygiene?

Think all the way down to...

xxi.

I don't want this to degenerate into a speciesist tract, but the whisper-snickered tattles about you-know-whom eating with their faces and wiping their assholes with both hands must contain a kernel, or maybe an undigested peanut, of truth.

This idiosyncratic state of impersonally hygienic affairs has a direct bearing on why our mini-ecosystem is peculiarly suited to this relgio-ethnicity, and why they permitted themselves to be heli-migrated here in such numbers in the first place.

Like the protopaleolithic-type wretches they were when originally condemned to total species-expungement in scato-scriptural days, they remain hunty-gathery at core. (Though, come to think of it, from what position do I condescend, having been reduced to that level myself, or at least the latter half of the job description?) Their proud yet squalidly nomadic culture never invented anything like a syllabary, so paper never entered their so-called "minds." Therefore, neither did that superfluous luxuriance of civilization come near their opposite ends.

So they require handfuls of greenery to be perpetually poised at the ready, tickling up between their struthious legs, to aid in the two-fisted de-chunkification of whatever shoddy apparatus their Creator, Jawhey (himself indifferently configured), has bothered to plumb for them by way of a nether-vent. Sometimes, as I ponder our foreign guests from a few paces off, I wonder if they can truly be said to have crotches any more than oral cavities.

Can it truly be called a crotch?

This has resulted in the famously exotic custom, which is known abroad as the—

Middlingly Oriental Grass Wipe

It has come popularly to symbolize their entire presence on the planet, just as kindergartens full of type-two diabetics stereotypify a certain other civilization which will remain shameless.

The on-the-hoof running grass-wipe is doubly piquant as a behavior because, back in the occupied territories of their home-sand, even before we smote them and our Flamma-Manna settled whitely down to liquefy the olive-drab skins of their siblettes, stands of grass were as few and far-flung as bubbly oases. Now we have debiologized the place, the above statement can be italicized and indented even more emphatically.

So, where they've lived for seven thousand years, the chance to wipe one's ass has always

the riverside where they've roamed
for seven thousand years...

a stand of date palms
in the middle of a hypoglycemic jag

been a real treat, the equivalent of stumbling upon a stand of date palms in the middle of a hypoglycemic jag. Finding themselves heli-dumped charitably down to a such a grassy eco-niche, our visitants believe they've been translated whole to Ornitho-Plantigrade Viparoid Heaven and laved in six hundred houri-hens' copulation sauces, without even suiciding for the privilege.

Their marvelously pullulizing extrusion of carbon not only promotes the growth of the Flyblown Fruiting Body at home, but it brings forth the occasional marvel of life on the otherwise hermetically sterile grit of the far Judeuphrates bank. The Amalekite ethnicity truly is autochthonous, literally one with its native soil, for there would be no soil without them. To the impious crypto-Darwininst, it would no doubt reduce to a pullet-ovum paradox.

Everyone else will begin to see, on pondering the purity of this symbiosis, the depth and extent of our crime. We have been destructive to a source of calories as well as clean crotches. We have violated nature, nutrition and hygiene as well. One can see why Dad—who, in his youth, helped hawk our weapon in this felony—is attempting to atone by riding at the head of their mounted resistance, doomed as it is.

* * * *

Hunty-gathery Bedou-types prematurely introduced to the sedentary existence of the municipality put on weight and grow louche. They succumb to luxuriation and become decadent and socially graceless. With the corruption of civil lawns comes inclemency of speech and ingratitude toward the host. Hence their mean mitt wiggles, which our kennel fodder was purchased to bark off, but does not. The relict chicks, in particular, are always dactylogizing something bitchy at me.

Their handed babble comes off grammatically and lexically quaint, even though most of them possess what appears to be an authentic pollex opposed on their innermost forelimbs. (Only we amongst higher mammaloids come by that digit honestly, as a non-enriched choco-covered

refugeniks' dialect coach

plutonium shell-induced mutation.) Their locutions are stylistically influenced by the hiatally belched cretino-rap of our Sovereign Ecclesiarchy's disaffected blight mall-crawling Talibangers.

As I try to scrape up a few calories for my family I am rapped on the knuckles with such free verse as—

"Look with derisive laughter upon the litter-runt who in probability conceals a vulvesque homologue under the strapless prom gown which, while thick in fiber and subtropical in batik, is inappropriately effeminate!"

—and—

"Scorn with cruelty the sister boy's beehive hair stylings, complete with insect life! He, no doubt, maestrobates!"

The stinkingest garbage of our culture oozes through our porous borders and osmoses across the laterally monotidal and saltless sea that protects us but nobody else. Backyard refugeniks embrace melano-Taligang couture, but disdain Mom's love-sarongs, and mock them when they appear off my shoulders. I take this as nothing other than a warm recommendation. Her aesthetic is far too refined to filter down to third-world heli-migrant grass wipers. They scoffed, too, at the fashionable boa she improvised from the integumentary appendages of the first dumb beast they subverted.

This in spite of the fact that I water down my 'do and switch to dungarees before going out to scavenge subsistence, and rarely, if ever, maestrobate in within their shot. This indicates to me that the wretches have been not only peeking, but listening and, ominously enough, comprehending through the aperture of that particular blind sac in our house-bowel called the "dining room"—ironically enough, for that's where Mom drains psychergy from my siblette and is trying to consume soul nutrition off me as well.

And it turns out, theirs is a stench phonetics, engaging not manual postures so much as the rich, ripe miasma thereof. Being animalistic themselves, they have been able to use, not paw patois so much as mitt hogo, eloquently enough to turn Hildegard von Bingo's elongated head with silent schmoozing.

Hence my lack of an affectionate center of hardly more than rudimentary consciousness to commiserate with, to help me unloose pressure, to postpone the love explosion I earlier spoke of, which will end with either me or Mom getting metabolized, with perhaps a few evidentiary flecks of connective tissue left the dining room rug. This romance in your hands may yet end so, because I vent no red steam from thrice daily auto-defenestration.

a few evidentiary flecks
of connective tissue on the dining room rug

xxii.

In a barely beyond fetal, half-hatched, irrecovered memory I contain a vague image of The Father Figure riding off into a dioxin-discolored sunset, or maybe dawn. He's ill-defined, a more or less apocalyptoid figure on a vintage ride, his mating/mayhem crest contracted to conform to the aerodynamics of a canter, seen from a distance hazed with motherly lies, unrequited daughterly embryo-lust and, of course, the blood-tinted outrage of our Sovereign Ecclesiarchy.

As per our Divinely Revealed Criminal Code, on a charge of blasphemo-treason in time of transriverine genocide, the Municipal Priestcrafters would like nothing better than to drag this relative of mine home, slit his belly just a tad, unspool his entrails through the tight hole, anoint them with holy astringent, then wrap them, love-sarong-wise, to pucker and contract around his neck in the sun—assuming a glint or two of the latter resource can be persuaded to glint between billows of our theocracy's frankinsensual smogma.

Though our creed, race, state, tribe, culture, affectations, fads, language, preferential sexualities and landmass are coextensively coterminous, and though qualification for our baptizenship is neither more nor less than chromosomal, the influx of displaced mutants and their mushroom-friendly excrement, scented with such sheer alienness, has filled our bellies, cross-fertilizing us, like Melanogroids fetching their muscled bongos northward to vitalize the effete medleys of the Carcinomians.

Yes, the Relict Amalekites emphatically remain our propinquitoidal kithkin. Hence, I suppose it's possible to recognize the poetic justice of the execution method proposed for turncoats like Dad, when the coat they turn, both inside and out, is tailored of the Others', and our, mutual epidermis. Since oneself is being forsaken in every sense of the word, why not be throttled by one's own innards?

I undergo this very punishment in bimonthly dreams which surprise me with their solidarity for someone I have never, and will never meet. Like pendulum clockwork, I drape myself in Father's love-sarong.

* * * *

Here is the real reason why we eat off our own soil—and it has less to do with agrarian solidarity than craven agoraphobia. It's too miserable visiting the food court at the blight mall, or any other public place for that matter. To the greater world of the Riparian Megalopolis we are nothing more or

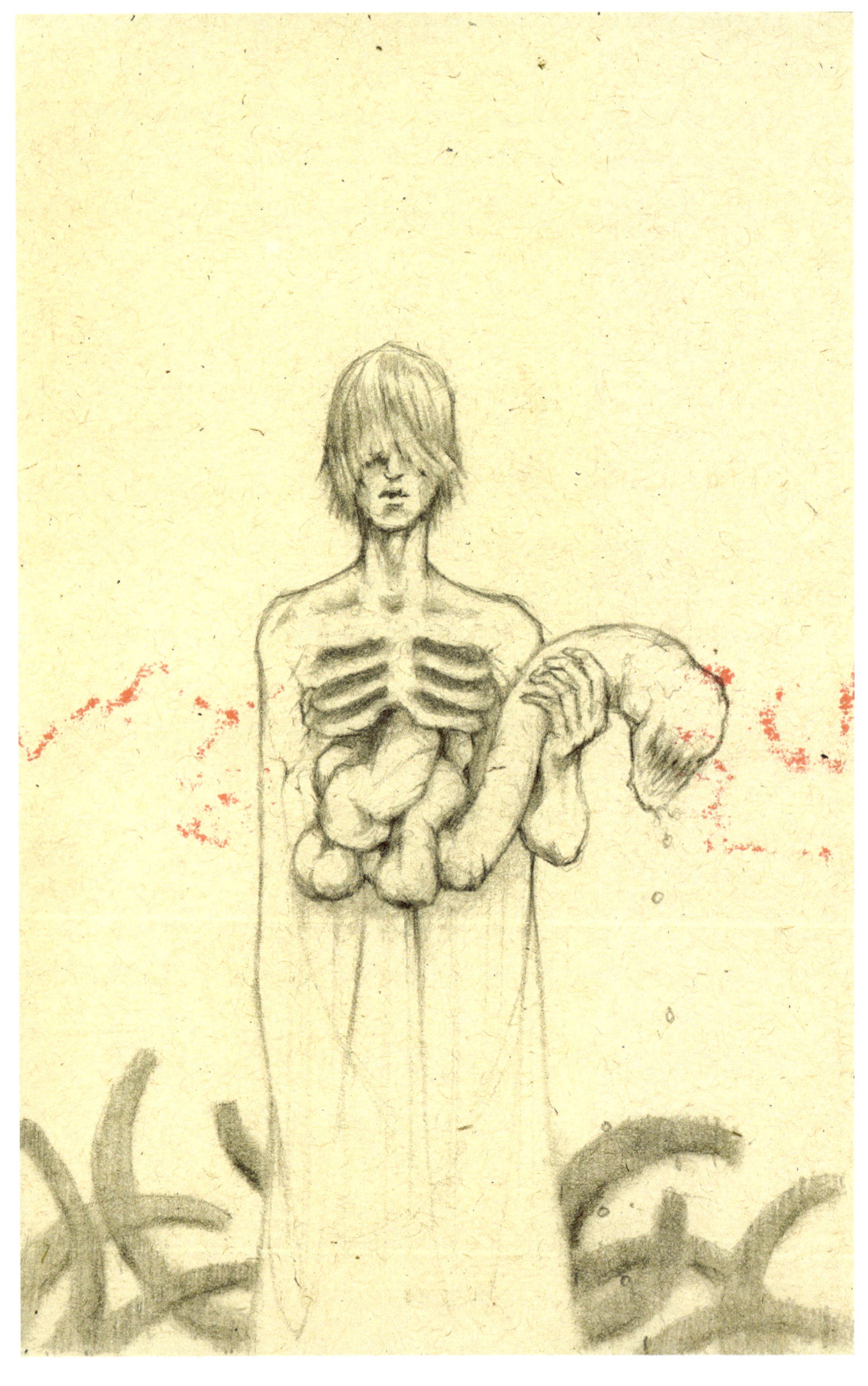

I drape myself in my father's love-sarong.

less than the grotesque detritus of a heretic/deserter who helps idolatrous infidels riot obstreperously in a savage locale.

A loyal member of our family (if there was one) would be obliged to point out to these neighborhood gossips that, according to the revealed Relict Amalekite scato-scriptures, Jawhey personally secreted the pertinent waterway on the Twelfth Day of Creativousness, and coagulated its far bank to serve as those idolaters' rightful perma-turf, not a proving ground for our latest murder products.

(Although, come to think of it, if that is the case, and if this ostensible Jawhey is also responsible for having random-rigged their fundaments, one wonders why he didn't supply the underfooting with more plentiful provender for the Middlingly Oriental Grass Wipe.)

I can offer you an exercise if you want to gauge the refugeniks' intellectual capacities. Try reminding them that their pod of undocumented mopes just happened to be heli-barfed at the periphery of a household whose former head is at this moment selflessly attempting to win them back their home-sand, thereby condemning himself either to perpetual exile or to execution. Try pointing out to these ingrates that their absentee landlord traversed their precious ancestral Judeuphrates to link up with their coreligionists' resistance (measly as it is), and they should be worshipful toward us rather than getting all snickery when looking and listenting in upon our chamber of mycophagia.

I invite you to gauge their facial expressions when being informed of this shameful irony. None whatsoever.

XXiii.

In my foraging mode, as I tiptoe unobtrusively as possible to gather our familistic breakfast, lunch, sacramental snack, and dinner, I always worry that I'm about to be grabbed with dirty-talking hands and called a certain two-syllable bad name that gets under my skin more effectively than the worst Mom bug.

There is a third sex amongst our resident fertilizers, whom I call The Jocks, for lack of an even more nearly perfect name. At rest they are indistinguishable from the females. But, under duress or sadistic excitement, also during the metamorpho-molting season, they are peculiarly adapted, in the name of dissimulation and camouflage, to retract their shoulder teeth and suck in the trilobite shells which define their phylum. These structures, upon retraction, pucker into a roughly prosimian physiognomy, like a Mom-style pathogen with its falsely eye-spotted wings. A sort of head-like knob is just incidentally formed by the wads and folds of puckered exoskeleton, upon which, as if in some dim bestial mimicry of the mating/mayhem crest displayed by higher species, they will plop the latest chapeau from the Talibanger boutique in the Riparian Megalopolis' blight mall.

It's a form of aping worthy of an illuminated panel in the crypto-Darwinizer's black-magical bestiary. At these times they come uncannily to resemble the worst sick-maker Mom herself ever hallucinated and sicced upon our coiffures, as if in her mock-maternal sado-anxiety she was actually trying to teach us a geopolitical pathogenophobia. The unwellness they vector is digital rupture of the

There is a third sex.

sclera, the goosing of the retinae.

Through their provisional mouthish mimesis the Jocks are able, like parrots, more or less mindlessly to mimic speech, but no more than a couple of syllables per mouthful. Under such quasi-linguifying metamorphoses their fingers are freed up for more emphatic forms of ideational transfer.

Their peculiar grass-wiped uncrotchedness remains as a telltale sign that no true transpeciation has occurred, only the dissembling of the octopus or chameleon, with their anal vents staying in place at the base of what would be the sternum, were such misshapen botches equipped with rib cages in the first place.

The list of primitive tricks these bullies learned from our disaffected melano-youth includes, when they want to express particularly emphatic notions, the use of the middle and forefingers as eyeball gougers. All I can say is squinch your lids like sphincters in a locker room.

the worst she ever hallucinated

This is called the internationalization of culture, and we have been instructed to take pride in it, as our rim of the runny border is a Fondue Pot for all manner of miscegeno-cheesiness. Anyone whose world we occupy and render uninhabitable is welcome to relocate here and enjoy sub-baptizen status, assuming they have survived the Flamma-Manna which we cause to fall on their "corrupt dictators"—which is what we call any tribal elders, sacerdotal authorities, grandmas, etc., who happen to enjoy bigger than average hovels.

The tertiarily gendered Jocks call me a certain bad name which, given the nature of my hereditary hypochondria and lifelong dietary behavior, could not be better calculated to grate on my soul like ragged fingernails on a Flamma-Manna blister. It won't be repeated here, this epithetic hideosity. But when I slip into their midst these bad imitation Talibangers call me out, as follows:

"You're not bearing much resemblance to your male parent, are you? Unlike you, he flung off yo' mau-mau's decolletaged promenade night-ie. He fights over the waterway to liberate our most superantiquated cradle of civics. It appears as though heroism skips a generation in your evolutionary nook."

XXiv.

How am I to reply? Like most expatriates, they're pathetically out of touch with current events. Have a look at Dad's latest secret letter from the "most superantiquated cradle" which my tormentors couldn't wait to escape. Pay particular heed to the first ominous octet of words—

Your begetter's inevitable comeback is in the offing.

I'm violating the fluid frontier for the second time in my life, now in the opposite direction, un-mounted.

I have turned my odd-toed ungulate out to pasture in the sand—a stud if there ever was one, with struts and rivets to augment the studs.

Dad's permanent distension.

I no longer need the ride I rode instead of my bride, because—as you well know—I have an ultimate mount waiting on your side of the river,

welcoming party

a center of consciousness to centaur myself onto, whom I can depend on, once and for all, forever.

Stand by for that, my colt.

I'm getting old. Just as the backs of patriarchal bonobos get silver, so do the mating/mayhem crests of us aging Cavalrymen become permanently engorged, distended at full display. This is a reverse irony, geronto-priapically speaking, a literal yet belated horniness.

I'm coming to meet that big deadline we all face, yes. But in this case it will come in a final cis-Judeuphratic struggle, a hand-to-hand pugnacity, with none other than the Highest of High Physio-Functionaries who licked the peace symbol between my shoulder blades, time gone by, and more recently cunnilingua-strappadoed my filly: the Grand Religio-fucking-asshole-etcetera.

* * * *

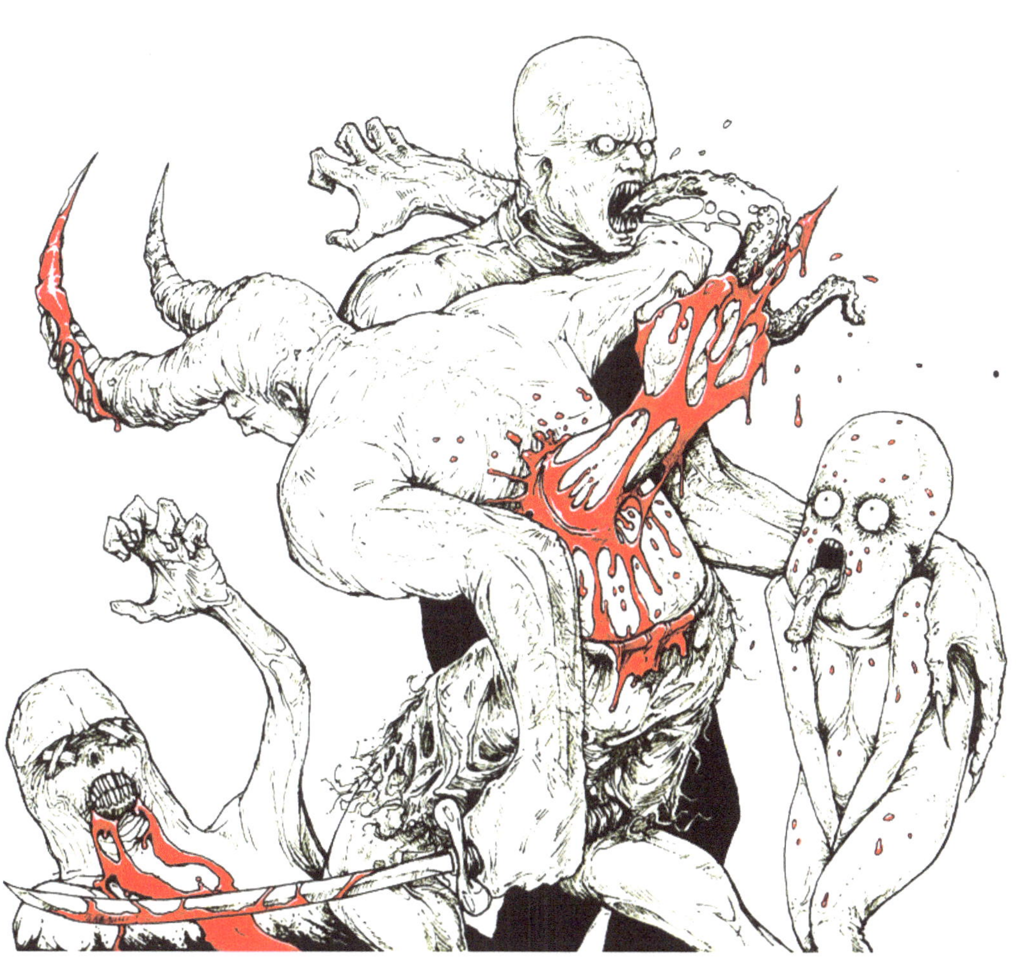

*In the big climactic showdown,
new meaning is lent to the term "fisting."*

And guess who observes my father's prog-ress from a cliff on this bank, tongue writhing with anticipation of waxy bouquet. True to his reputa-tion for honor, the asshole has brought his brace of ordained heavies, plus a backup, stacking the odds.

I wish it were more—I don't know—emo-tional or something. But I hardly knew either guy.

*What follows is not so much
a struggle as a metabolization.*

XXV.

Talking of the religiose letch and the One Special Foremost Fear it is supposed to band-aid over, I suppose I have to make it explicit. Our attenuated clan has experienced limb-loss, ghost pain. Dad is dead. He's a—

dead dad.

And I bet, having heard that, you've already guessed it's not just with eye-spotted entomology that our quondam-puerpera exerts her will on our upper-respiratory tracts. She hijacks our weep-sniffles as well, or what is more sensitively called "the grieving process."

After sulking through an unexpected, yet brief moment of strange blue catatonia—which I choose to interpret as a distorted form of sadness—she got her dander back up and commenced with the usual bare-naked mycosophic hyper-pietism. Her way of sublimating spousal bereavement is to go all Priestess-crafty on us.

Dad's homecoming-cum-equestriexequy was celebrated in the backyard. And guess who performed as mourners and pallbearers. I suppose, in their animalistic way, our guests did vaguely consider him their national hero. But I got the impression Mom engaged their services in return for scavenging rights afterward.

Our household has harbored a Cassandra all this time. What appeared, these many years, merely to be Sissy's schizoid hallucination of Dad's bedungeonment in the backyard, turned out to be nothing less than time-leaping precognition.

Mom went all Priestess-crafty on us.

We sank him in the shit of the beings whose stay-at-home cousins he failed to save from live skeletalization.

in return for services rendered

* * * *

Mom's vulvic behavior at the send-off grossed me out, to such an extent that, afterwards, I repaired to my room, where (after checking the ceiling for

No, she likes it.

No, she likes it.

any progenitrices suction-cupped to the sheetrock), I shed my love-sarong, along with every tonsorial permutation, till my skin and scalp were bare as the divine Krystelle Rex's, and I expressed my unhappiness by means of breather-hole.

Do you think the noise might bother Maniac Mater as she lies, bored, yawning, butt-scratching, in her chamber directly overhead? No, she likes such music. She calls it "Her little Dudamel rehearsing woodwinds instead of percussion for a change."

She has as good as amputated my hands, Krystelle Rexing me to the wrists, and robbed my ability even to maestrobate in lightlessness. Is it a wonder I howl like a monkey?

I don't think she understands that I am preparing myself for a certain genetic function here.

her vulvic behavior

XXVI.

If such a burlesque Dad send-off causes comparatively stable me to howl in my room, it amounts to the cruelest mistreatment of his daughter. She goes all but catatonic to see her worst fears of paternal interment carried out—overseen by her own family, no less.

Then she snaps out of it and becomes irritating. She takes up her dolly-wolly and gambols one too many times around the food table, to inexpressibly hideous effect.

Mom's concerned that our resident anorexic might not remain in this perpetual state of arrested

Sissy mustn't look Mom in the eye.

development. The child could respond to bereavement with growth; and grown daughters tend to see mothers as they truly are, looking them right in the death-bound eye. That will never do. So a certain Qualified Medical Professional must be house-called in.

Since visiting our home the last time, crusty Ol' Doc Clyster, our familistic comic relief, has coincidentally been pondering this very problem. His head already bursting full with erudition, he has developed an unorthodox technique to ensure that he will never learn from his numerous clinical errors and diagnostic missteps. This also saves money on kerosene and kindling, and is easier on the envirulence—at least till potty time, which, as with so many of our senior citifieds, rolls around infrequently enough, especially in the doc's case. Besides, recycling body parts and allowing stem cells to alight, unsecured, in a dumpster runs contra to our clerisy's spiritual queasiness.

So, with full parental blessing and urging, he determines that my sister constitutes a medical waste disposal problem.

But, having been world-class bulemic ever since Winfrey's memorial meal, Siblette transmits to him the Seven-Course Achoo, the Whole-Grain Gesundheit pathogen, and is back in a splash.

The Seven-Course Achoo reprised;
the Whole-Grain Gesundheit, again

XXVII.

My suspicions about parthenogenesis have become certainties. The only thing I wonder now is whether there's a seam. Was there ever discontinuity between me and my former host twin? Maybe Mom has become the overdue growth on my back which corresponds to the one she herself displays when suiting up for thanato-estrus.

Am I Mom's former warty outgrowth, an ex-ball of hair and teeth that sprouted like a pus-distended lymph node in the left armpit of her doubly prehensile hump? If so, our virgin relationship would conduce to reabsorption, one parasite turning

Mom won't stop bleeding over my shoulder.

the tables on the other. She is Abigail to my Britney, my prehensile Hensel.

Parthenogenesis would explain the uncanny control she's always had over me—and my ability, no less uncanny, to turn that around on her, like a river caused to flow uphill in scato-scripture. This pertains to the inevitable moment when the yoked pair of us will revert and convert and pervert until she's but a graft on my own shapely shoulders—for I am firstborn Cavalry.

* * * *

With our household dysfunctioning all around me in puddles, I try to do a little escapist reading. I attempt to take in Blurt Vomitgut, but the red and black widow tries to distract me. She fears I'll read the true nature of unwellness vectors, and learn that she, herself, is the virulent one that has lit on me.

I can feel her thighs. She's reading over my shoulder, bleeding over my shoulder, forcing her post-menopausality to blend with the Blurt-Man's ficto-homiletic textures. Literacy is a struggle for some folks; integration of the corpus is a struggle for others.

medical waste disposal

The fresh widow, who should be in her weeds, would appear to be Lady Paramount of this domestic scene; but it's an exchange of body fluids. Some of the sauce is osmosing counter-gravitationally. I dissolve her. This is her death scene, not mine. I am doing a Stevie Daedalus. I whole-head orgasm her off in a Sneeze Megacatastrophic.

When I absorb Mom—or, at any rate, a pretty hefty chunk of her, like a weakened pathogen, it amounts to incestuous homeopathy. It's only logical for Doc Clyster to make one final house call and dispose of the waste from my self-medication.

XXViii.

Nobody remains in the house but you-know-who and me.

Somewhat risen out of her regressive mode, having shed or maybe eaten her dolly-wolly, and grown back several of her scalp filaments, she stands sentry at the dining room window. The refugeniks cannot eavesdrop and mock with their logorrheic digits because she, who comprises my whole family now, holds them at bay with nothing but her general air of unwholesomeness. Act like a sick spook and they shy away, for they are superstitious.

All other windows have been absorbed like tumors with no blood vessels to feed them. Doors and remaining domicilic apertures have been atomized, laser-scalpeled away, their holes healed over with patterned cicatrices. All that remains is the wallpaper, the ceilingpaper, a Blakean cubicle.

I am displaying my physical and moral subsumption of dead Mom's doubly prehensile hump, as morphed with dead Dad's inflamed mating/mayhem crest. The latter personage is reconnoitering, not reading, over my shoulder. He rides his rightful heir with all the cooperative dependency of a crack Cavalryman. His postmortem strength is poised at the ready if required.

Thus I have absorbed both forebears. I have rolled my love sarong off the shoulders and down to where it rides like a fluid surface that renders the genital configuration ambiguous, making of me a salvific Papa pube-deep in oubliette drainage—paralleling the execution swaddle of Krystelle Rex in throes of splatter-iconic passion. My nakedness

holding off the eavesdroppers with
nothing but her general air
of unwholesomeness

is that of a selfless saddle straddling soldier breaking the Judeuphrates.

A river is made of the garment forced on me by natal circumstance. Yes, it's a skirt, but the Mommishness is made mine. Similarly, my hair choice indicates that I have not been enwrapped by the villainess of this romance, but have contained her. Yes, I sport a fem-'do, but it's my own stylization: the teased beehive, devoid of eye-spots.

I have put on the most fashionable wrap-around garment in Mater's dank closet. So as not to distract your eyes with mutual revulso-magnetism (we've both ogled long and hard enough as it is), my own orbs have not been jabbed by the pins of her neuterine brooches, but wrapped with a rag, thick in fiber, ripped from her own rarely donned love sarong. She has blinded, but not spayed me like an attack-mammaloid. She has caused the mistaken pair of balls to be scooped.

Dad rides again.

My head is so tightly bound to keep it from exploding in case I sneeze, encircled with a blindfold, a hovering doughnut of a Saturn halo, a mobius tiara. And, disinfection and integration having been simultaneously encompassed, note the absence of perchers and nesters up there: no causatives of the Disastrous Achoo to smear physiognomy around the room in a black and red mist.

I am recollecting emotion in tranquility, leaving an account book to be deposited, buried Qumran-wise, among the evacuated rubbly detritus of our exploded Romantic Family, deep under feathery turds.

It is only when Dad's letters keep arriving that I realize how such lethally seditious mail has been getting through to me. There was no foolhardy, suicidal or bribed postman involved. The paternal epistles were my very own hallucinations all along, self-addressed if not stamped. They've been expressions of my literary bent, my inner ficto-homilist waiting to come to consciousness with

Dad's return home in a box. I have blurted and vomited my own guts all along.

Dressed like Krystelle Rex, equipped with stylus like his rival-twin-other self, I have subsumed both halves of the shizo-god, brought integrity to Jawhey and his effete outgrowth. I'm not so much a literatus as a slinger of graphic abstractions via the stylus—in this way I take on the attributes of my trans-Judeuphratic cousins' tutelary.

If you want this graphic item to murmur in your right ear, or your left or your inner-, you need to master some hieroglyphs. Not Chinese or Egyptian, but the kind scraped on hot sandstone cliffs by accident of wind and water. You want the kind of ideo-paleographs that require a wide expanse so they can be silently spoken with a broad sweep.

Observe the never-before-seen yet uncannily familiar calligraphy with which I, in a virtuoso flourish of one massive yet delicate hand, beautify the Scroll of Flowing Beauty, this final apotheosis of your narrator as artificer, this—

ekphrastic auto-evocation, this sheer ecstatic hermaphrodisiac spasm of bimegalomania.

Critical

Appendices

Critical Appendex A

by John-Ivan Palmer,
author of *Master of Deception*

Family Romance is the seventeenth of thirty books by Tom Bradley, the notorious hermit of Kitakyushu, Japan. It's a monstrosity of the imagination, as if a Burroughs virus hijacked the machinery of *Finnegans Wake* and replicated itself as a litera-teratus. Illustrator Nick Patterson joins Bradley in the procedure with a hundred disturbing images of Bosch-like detail you don't want to see on the way home from your local head shop.

Bradley's trajectory of books, from the early Sam Edwine novels up through the mesmeric satire of *Vital Fluid* and essay collections like *Put It Down In A Book*, is toward a geist where categories have yet to be described. The fastenings and joineries of his new textual and graphic ubiety are measured in calibrations from some other dimension where the usual sockets and taper points of critical disassembly have to be replaced. Even with that, *Family Romance* is deviously structured to lead conclusion jumpers straight to the Hall of Laughter.

By way of guidance I might advise the intrepid reader to follow first the theme of mutation, both in the nameless family the book portrays and the language that describes it. There's a father, mother, daughter and son. And don't forget the dog. The narrator is the son who combines self-image and family dynamics with this rhetorical question: "Am I Mom's former wart, an ex-ball of hair and teeth that sprouted like a pus-distended lymph node in the left armpit of her doubly prehensile arm?" Mom herself is "the fascist conjuress" who "scrounges the means to bring about lovely coiffures high upon our occupied heads, all the better for her unwellness vectors to perch and nest." Anything you can relate to? Or how about dear old Dad, "born with a cavalryman's plasma osmosing through his various connective tissues... his inborn lot in civic-caste life."

So there you have it, parents in a military family "meant to kill and explode things, not frisk and frolic." Military families are known to have military brats like the narrator himself, or his un-hinged sister, "a trans-species facial-fornicatory bastardette" and victim of degenerate "priestcraft-ers," who constitutes nothing more than "a medi-cal waste problem." Sib rivalry? And then the dog. Well, the dog doesn't do too well either.

The father deserts the family. He turncoats his post and joins a foreign insurgency in the "Mid-dlingly Oriental homeland." One thinks right away of the Palestinians or the Muslim umma, but in *Family Romance* things can mutate before you get to the end of the analogy. Mother raises the kids in the father's absence and tries to keep them clean. Clean of what? Pathogens! A pathogen in this con-text is both an organism and a meme, always the other guy's. Infection with memic thought disorder fractures the family, as it often does, along religious lines. Mom buys into a "national-racial god" known as "the divine Krystelle Rex" (sounds like crystal meth?). Dad gangs up with the biblical-sounding "Relic Amalekites" on the "Judeuphrates."

I'm going to make the astonishing assertion that *Family Romance* is a work of theology, if by theology we mean cryptophagic religious chagrin. Biblical quotes turn up frequently in epigraphs to Bradley's fiction and non-fiction where he dwells, sometimes in great Talmudic depth, on themes of sin, atonement, transcendence, holiness, Gnosticism and Mesopotamian history. You can jaw away your lauds on Bradley's concept of Jawhey (Yahweh) who, "in the septafold naves of his cathedralic heart... suppurates a special letch for Relic Amalekites." And the Relic Amalekites "are the self-styled Originally Selected Beings of this particular god, whom they adore and reverence as the Unitary Executive and Decider of the Present Solar Clump." If it's a clue to anything, the Amelakites, mentioned in the book's epigraph from I Samuel, were one of the ancient enemies of Israel, with no evidence of existing anywhere outside the Old Testament. I'm not sure if this leads to grace or the Hall of Laughter.

I'll try another approach. There are three generations of Mormons in Bradley's own family and he has viciously excoriated their belief system (see chapter six of *Fission Among the Fanatics* before you send money to Mitt Romney). That may account for the distressed credos. I'd also aver that his preoccupation with teretogenic effects is from growing up in Utah downwind from nuclear test sights in Nevada, furthered by his current exile only a few train stops from Nagasaki (where he was an English professor until drummed out for mutating the syllabus). Parthogenesis of thought, as well as body from nuclear radiation, runs through much of Bradley's work, especially in *Bomb Baby*, itself textually mutated from the novel *Kara-Kun* from his *Dai-Nippon Trilogy*.

Family Romance may best be read within its own self-extruded scutum, beginning with the title. A romance is traditionally defined as an entertainment, and there's plenty of that in Nick Patterson's haunting illustrations of robotoids and autotrophs crawling out of tar pits. There's much to enjoy in Bradley's wordplay, such as describing toadstools as "the albino kind that hickeys lightless cave walls." There's stand-up comedy of the Martin Amis sort: "Talk about tattoo regret: trendy unblood-lust outpacing subcutaneous discolor." By definition, the romance occurs in worlds (or word labs) far removed from the everyday. Its characters perform spectacular if not heroic deeds, in Bradley's case, like whole-head engulfment of someone else's genome. Finally, there's a practical ending to *Family Romance*, which satisfies the form's didactic requirement.

This book is not for those who pick their reading from eye-level in the check-out line, although for all its linguistic twistages it's easier to read than you might expect. At one point the narrator advises you to stop reading and engage in "an eight to twelve hour introspection... and look inside the stacked deck called yourself." If you're good at speed introspection this might take only a few moments. It might take longer to master the suggested hieroglyphics, "the kind scraped on hot sandstone cliffs by accident of wind." Whichever way you digest it, this bizarre story is ultimately a prophylaxis to thought perversion, the kind that results in the dreaded "Sneeze Catastrophic" that can blow off the whole front of your face.

Critical Appendex B

by James Kendley,
author of *The Wine Ghost*

Kendley Fiction confirms it: Bizarro fabulist Tom Bradley exists, and he appears to be entirely human.

Taller than most, and much redder, but still.

I know Bradley exists because I've seen him. He taught alongside me at a Japanese institution of higher learning in the mid-nineties, and I spotted him at a spring semester start-up confab. This was a seasonal ritual in which *gaijin* EFL instructors reassured a harried consortium secretary that they could dress themselves, show up on time, and remain more-or-less sober during short presentations.

We played Japanese. It was fun! We smiled and bowed and sat in neat rows. The secretary was pleased. Everything was great.

Then came a ginger giant in a voluminous Hawaiian shirt. He made it clear that the whole thing was a crock of shit, a complete waste of his time. He split the second it was over, leaving the rest of us standing forlorn in our cheap Korean suits.

Months later, my mentor at that college told me of a manuscript received from a colleague. *Tom Bradley*, he called this colleague. A tall fellow…

"And red?" I asked tremulously. "Very red, favoring shirts Hawaiian and floral?"

It was so. Bradley's manuscript had displeased my mentor, who declined to pass it along to a friend at the William Morris Agency.

"It just wasn't my cup of meat," he said, employing a conflation of aphorism and euphemism he had used to great effect in his own manuscript, *Let's Practice Colloquial English.*

Time passed: I returned to the States with Renée, my honeycrunch Canadienne; my mentor hunkered down to spawn in the jungles of darkest Siam; and Tom Bradley emerged as the *inakamono* anchorite godfather of Bizarro letters.

Now, three decades later and half a world away, I can say without qualification that Tom Bradley's *Family Romance* is Kendley Fiction's cup of meat.

Even the initial premise is irresistible: Nick Patterson provided a hundred illustrations, and Bradley wove among them a tale of life under an industrialized, militaristic theocracy dedicated to the genocide of the relic Amalekites, wretches cursed by Jehovah in the first book of Samuel way back in the porno-scriptural times before whatever Big Thing brought us to this point, said genocide undertaken in order to recover the Weapon of Sparse Destruction allegedly developed by said relic Amalekites.

Our narrator, growing up in the shadow of an absent father, resides in urban catastrophe on the banks of the Judeuphrates River with his sister (nearly catatonic thanks to the tender ministrations of the Grand Religiopath and/or his minions) and Mom.

Four ways to read *Family Romance*:
1) an ironically pseudo-semi-autobiographical take on boyhood in Utah during the age of above-ground H-bomb testing, perhaps Bradley blowing

off steam left over from *Fission Among the Fanatics*,

2) a scathing allegorical satire of modern America gone off the rails in a jingoistic, genocidal frenzy of right-wing Christian extremism,

3) an extended and elaborate Rorschach test in which we examine the relationships between Patterson's disturbing stimuli and Bradley's horrifying, outrageously funny responses,

4) or a heartwarming coming-of-age story.

Take your pick.

The real point of reading Bradley, aside from his illumination of the ridiculous and grotesque world around us, is the rolling cadence of his pitch-perfect writing. We prize competent prose here at Kendley Fiction, but we absolutely adore Bradley's strong, steady voice guiding us with spot-on verbiage and heady switchbacks to revelations by turns disgusting, divine, and gut-bustingly hilarious.

He's always a treat, and knowing that Nick Patterson's drawings came first gives us a little more insight into the mind of Tom Bradley (see option 3, above). Presented with these disturbing and downright frightening illustrations, why did Bradley choose this direction for his narrative?

• A Relic Amalekite cleansing its fundament with tufts of tall grass — yup. What else would this illustration portray, now that I read the text?

• Mom employing "her formidable vagina to point out the superior vertebral development of her urban assault vehicle" — check.

• This illustration engenders the phrases "Sneeze Catastrophic" and "off-the-shoulder love-sarongs."

Of course it does.

But who the hell would make those particular associations in the first place?

Bradley, that's who. He's one of a kind.

In the long run, our own reactions to *Family Romance* may be the greatest revelation of all. Learn more about Tom Bradley — and perhaps more about yourself as well, *liebchen*. Kendley Fiction guarantees that, at the very least, you will not, cannot, be neutral about *Family Romance*, our cup of meat.

Critical Appendex C

Cye Johan interviews Tom Bradley

CJ: How did *Family Romance* get made?

TB: In just the opposite way from most illustrated novels. Nick Patterson's hundred pictures came first, and I wrote the novel around, between, underneath and through them. One day I came upon a great stack of his artwork, and was instantaneously locked in. Each image presented a climactic moment in a strange, unspoken, yet definite story.

Nick's drawings and paintings are like the hallucinations of epileptic mystics as preserved in icons and illuminated hagiographies. They rear up in the aether before your eyes, bristling their spikes of light, needing no context but themselves. Yet they insist that a whole chronicle be imaginatively filled in, to perform the impossible task of explaining how these bizarreries came to be juxtaposed.

CJ: One of Nick Patterson's online fans asked him how he came up with his stuff, and he replied, "I pay attention to random thoughts."

TB: A perfect motto for him. That single sentence gives a vivid glimpse into the head of such a visual artist. We all have dreams and daydreams that are so utterly without rational context that they vanish before we can recall anything but the most general outlines. Even those dissolve within seconds. Nick not only remembers all, but he draws it in meticulous detail. He gives a perfect anatomical rendering of something that never had anatomy in the first place, at least not on this plane of forms.

For example, in Chapter One of *Family Romance*, a giant moth has fastened onto the narrator's head. In context, it seems natural and inevitable that such a drastic pathogen would cause his face to explode in a catastrophic sneeze: scarlet gore, brain matter and eye jelly everywhere. And, of course, anyone familiar with the pneumatics of a physical body will tell you that such a traumatic shock will cause the muscles, connective tissues and blood vessels of his neck and shoulders to throb, swell, writhe—all drawn here to exacting clinical perfection.

It's a strange picture, for sure—and yet, the strangest part is not the physiology, but the fashion. Look at the garment he's wearing. Where the fuck did that come from? The style, the fabric: our novel starts with that article of clothing. Many of Nick's figures, the weak and strong, the beautiful as well as horrendous, wear this same peculiar kind of wrap-around sarong, pulled high or low on the torso, depending, it seems, on the moral and/or emotional condition of the wearer.

CJ: In keeping with the mystical iconographic mood, a couple of gods appear in the book. They remind me of mutated versions of the desert deities that have been the CEOs of our own world for such a long, miserable time.

TB: Definitely, they are both the jealous monotheistic type. Hence their rivalry. There's an Old Testament Jehovah figure, overbearing and monstrously snaggle-faced, and a species of Christ as well, who obeys the dress code. His sarong is pulled down around his pubis, to humiliate him when he's in execution mode.

This leads to the notion of religious warfare. And, according to logic (external as well as internal), the theater of operations must be the sort of Levantine-style desert where religious pathology takes root.

A war needs innocent victims, and Nick doesn't disappoint. The Relic Amalekites are grotesqueries with shoulder teeth, problematic crotches, and ostrich legs. Like all hallucinations, they have spontaneously generated between your skull walls. And there can be no greater proximity than inside the reptilian cortex. So we get refugees from the conflict zone, squatters in our back yard, eavesdroppers at the back window of the residence in which abides and writhes the eponymous family of this romance.

Above all is sinister, ravenous, erotic Mom, the Kali-Avatar, the Tantric Initiatrix. Her means of exerting control over her family is immune system anxiety, the constant evocations of such pathogens as the giant moth on the head that brings the Sneeze Catastrophic. Nude and protean, Mom indulges a compulsion to mount other creatures. She feeds us a jejune diet consisting solely of psychoactive mushrooms, feigning eucharistic shamanism.

I won't spoil the plot. But Mom eventually winds up nothing more than a medical waste disposal problem. The ending is vastly and ecstatically affirmative. Nick Patterson can draw that kind of picture as well. But, like an Eleusinian initiate, you must live through the entire psychodrama and make it through to the light at the other end of our labyrinthine cave before you've earned the right to be edified by his sublime images.

Other Collaborative Books

by Tom Bradley and Nick Patterson

Useful Despair
as Taught to the Hemorrhaging Slave
of an Obese Eunuch

Elmer Crowley: a Katabasic Nekyia
(with David Aronson)

Felicia's Nose
(with Carol Novack)

The Church of Latter-Day Eugenics
(with Chris Kelso)

tombradley.org   nickdjp.com